MAYBE A
MERMAID

MAYBE A MERMAID

Josephine Cameron

Farrar Straus Giroux
New York

Farrar Straus Giroux Books for Young Readers
An imprint of Macmillan Publishing Group, LLC
175 Fifth Avenue, New York, NY 10010

Printed in the United States of America by LSC Communications,
Harrisonburg, Virginia
Designed by Christina Dacanay
First edition, 2019
1 3 5 7 9 10 8 6 4 2

mackids.com

Library of Congress Cataloging-in-Publication Data

Names: Cameron, Josephine, author.
Title: Maybe a mermaid / Josephine Cameron.
Description: First edition. | New York : Farrar Straus Giroux, 2019. |
    Summary: When her mother, who sells Beauty & the Bee cosmetics and
    drives a Beemobile, surprises soon-to-be sixth-grader Anthoni with a trip
    to the Showboat Resort, Anthoni plans to finally make a "True Blue Friend."
Identifiers: LCCN 2018020371 | ISBN 9780374306427 (hardcover)
Subjects: | CYAC: Friendship–Fiction. | Mothers and daughters–Fiction. |
    Resorts–Fiction.
Classification: LCC PZ7.1.C327 May 2019 | DDC [Fic]–dc23
LC record available at https://lccn.loc.gov/2018020371

Our books may be purchased in bulk for promotional, educational, or business
use. Please contact your local bookseller or the Macmillan Corporate and
Premium Sales Department at (800) 221-7945 ext. 5442 or by email at
MacmillanSpecialMarkets@macmillan.com.

For Kevin, who makes me laugh until my stomach hurts and always shows up when needed

CONTENTS

MAYBE A
MERMAID

PROLOGUE:
THE BEEMOBILE

I was seven when I took my first ride in the Beemobile. It was the most beautiful car I'd ever seen—a bright-yellow hybrid with sleek black stripes down the sides and fuzzy bee antennas bouncing around on top. A honeypot air freshener hung from the rearview mirror, and the minute I breathed in that sticky-sweet smell, I realized everything Mom had ever told me was true. If you set a goal, work hard, and stick to the plan, you, too, can win a car shaped like a bee.

The summer Mom won the Beemobile, we got to fly all the way from Chicago to St. Louis, Missouri, for the annual Beauty & the Bee convention. The awards ceremony was held in a hotel ballroom with gold flowers in loop-de-loops on the ceiling. Mom and I stood backstage

in matching yellow dresses while the CEO of Beauty &
the Bee gave a speech about how Mom's stick-to-itiveness
had helped her sell more honey-based beauty products
than anyone else in the Midwest region. I peeked out at
five hundred people fanning themselves in the audience,
and my knees turned to Jell-O.

"It doesn't matter if you feel brave. It matters if you
act brave," Mom whispered.

She took my hand, and we walked out onto the stage
slowly, one foot in front of the other, waving at the audience like we'd rehearsed. Mom's hand was shaky and
sweaty against my palm, but her hair glowed under the
lights like a superstar's.

When we got to the podium, the CEO held up a set
of keys and jangled them in the air.

"Young lady," she said to me. "Your mother has been
promoted to Chief Pollinator. Do you know what that
means?"

My tongue wouldn't work, but it didn't matter. All
five hundred people in the audience shouted the words
for me:

"BRAND . . . NEW . . . CAR!"

Mom and I made a spectacle of ourselves, jumping
around and screaming at the top of our lungs. We couldn't
help it. It was a great day.

* * *

After the trip, Mom and I didn't sit around and bask in the glory of her promotion. We got right to work on our next Five-Year Plan. We filled her whiteboard with sales goals, timelines, and Action Steps. We created a list of Next Hive Destinations and I put the pins on the map: Milwaukee, Indianapolis, Cleveland, Grand Rapids. The cities sounded exciting and exotic, guaranteed to be filled with new friends and adventures.

When everything was planned, Mom let me stand on a stool and erase the words "Chief Pollinator" from the GOAL section of the whiteboard. She spelled the new words slowly so I could write them one by one in my thick, uneven scrawl: "Queen Bee." The letters squeaked with promise.

Mom and I knew that the best way to reach a goal is to have a good incentive—a reward that you want so badly, you'll work extra hard to get it. The B&B reward for reaching Queen Bee status was a diamond honeybee with golden wings. It was so glitzy that in St. Louis we'd seen a woman in a red pantsuit cry buckets of tears when the CEO pinned it to her lapel. But next to her new Five-Year Plan, Mom didn't put up a picture of a diamond bee.

Instead, she taped up a dusty old postcard of a white building shaped like a boat sitting in a field of daisies. The building had a black smokestack and porthole windows, and a wide blue lake sparkled in the background.

On the deck of the boat, a smiling, pigtailed girl stood on her tiptoes and waved at the camera. Above her head, bright, happy letters announced:

The Showboat Resort: Where True Blue Friends Meet.

I turned the phrase around in my mind. It sounded old-fashioned and magical. Like a fairy tale. Goose bumps tingled down my arms.

"What is it?" I asked.

"Our new incentive," Mom said. "I put a deposit down today. To keep us on track."

I nodded. A deposit on an incentive is a deposit on success.

"We're going to live there?" It was the greatest idea I'd ever heard, but Mom shook her head.

"No," she said. "But in five years, when I get promoted to Queen Bee, we're going to spend summers there. Like I did when I was a girl."

"On the boat?"

"The Showboat."

Back then, there were a lot of things I didn't know.

I didn't know that the Beemobile's antennas would lose their fuzz or that the honey-orange air freshener smell could fade away. I didn't know that cars and Five-Year Plans sometimes fall apart. Or that moving to a different city and being the new girl in school every few months was nothing like an exotic adventure.

What I knew when I was seven was that I would find my True Blue Friend at a magical boat-shaped resort in a picture-postcard. And that driving around in a car shaped like a bee would never, ever get old.

1

OFF WITH THE OLD
AND ON WITH THE NEW

Mom threw her hands in the air and slapped them back on the steering wheel. "S'mores!" she cried. "I can't believe it's been twenty years since I had a s'more!"

We'd been driving for three and a half hours, and Mom could not stop talking about The Showboat, the family resort in Eagle Waters where she had the Best Summer of Her Life—six years in a row. She chattered on about the time her water-ski team pranked the new kid by putting his swimsuit in the freezer, and the campfire tale that was so scary it made her True Blue Friend, Mary Pepper, pee her pants.

"Did I tell you about the time we found a skunk in

the bathtub?" she asked. "A real live skunk. I screamed so loud someone called the fire department!"

"I've never had a s'more!" I said, and flipped a page in my issue of *Wolverine and the X-Men.* I hadn't stopped grinning since Mom had shown up in the parking lot of Milwaukee West Elementary, stuck her head out the window of the Beemobile, and yelled, "Off with the OLD, on with the NEW!" loud enough for half the school to hear.

I was so glad to be done with fifth grade, I almost didn't notice the country music blasting from the car radio. But I definitely noticed the back seat of the Beemobile—packed to the ceiling with all our stuff. I hugged my backpack and gaped at Mom.

"We're moving?" I asked. "Today? Right now?"

Mom gave me a happy poke in the arm as she put her foot on the gas and pulled out of the parking lot. "Surprise!" she said.

I shrugged. Wherever we were headed, it couldn't be lonelier than Milwaukee. I'd been there since March, and hardly anyone knew who I was. Even Mr. Smith still looked around at the boys when he called "Anthoni Gillis" for roll. I tried to remember the next spot on our list.

"Minneapolis?" I asked. I hoped we could get an apartment with a shower that didn't leak. Or a landlord who didn't stop by every few days to argue about electricity and rent.

"Nope."

"Duluth?"

Mom tried to make her face look deadpan, but the corners of her mouth kept sneaking up.

"How about . . . The Showboat Resort?" She said it like it was any boring old town. Akron, Ohio, or Grand Rapids, Michigan. "It should take about four hours to get there."

My jaw hung open and Mom's laughter burst out like it had been killing her to hold it in so long.

"You did it?" I asked. "You got promoted to Queen Bee? How?"

I'm not a Negative Nelly, but as far as I knew, we weren't anywhere near reaching our goal. Sales had been down, and we hadn't signed up a new Worker Bee in months. Lately, Mom had been so desperate she'd been crashing conferences at hotels, trying to recruit Worker Bees in between breakout sessions. My lips spread into a grin.

"Was it the air-conditioning conference?"

Mom took a breath and smiled. Her eyes were tired and puffy even though I knew she'd gone through two jars of B&B's Royal Radiance Eye Cream (made with Royal Jelly!) in the last month.

"I told you that was a good idea," she said. "Air-conditioning manufacturers care as much about looking nice as anyone else does."

I had a thousand questions: How many Worker Bees had she signed up? Fifty? We needed forty-five to reach Queen Bee. What did the CEO of Beauty & the Bee say? Were they going to fly us to St. Louis for another awards ceremony so they could pin Mom with a diamond bee?

Before I could ask any of them, relief hit me, and suddenly I couldn't stop laughing. It was like a comic book. For months, we'd been stuck at that moment when Wolverine's a goner, backed into a corner by a guy whose skin is impervious to metal, and you can't help but wonder if this really *is* the end. But I should have known. That dark, all-is-lost moment is exactly when Storm shows up with a tornado to save her friend and blast the enemy off the page.

The air-conditioning conference was our tornado.

"We can get take-out pizza again!" I said, and laughed some more because I hadn't even known until that minute that I cared about take-out pizza. "I can taste the pepperoni!"

Mom fiddled with her earring and gave me a funny look.

"You okay?" I asked.

"Of course! I just . . . It's overwhelming, you know?"

"I know," I said. "You worked really hard."

Mom reached over and squeezed my knee. "WE worked really hard."

"True." I did a robot dance in my seat to make her laugh. "I *am* the best promotional products packer on the planet."

"Ha!" Mom turned the radio to earsplitting volume. Just the way we like it.

"When the going gets tough, the tough get going!" she shouted. "And we're going to The Showboat to have the Best Summer of Our Lives!"

2

NEXT HIVE DESTINATION: EAGLE WATERS

The website for The Showboat Resort hadn't changed one bit since I was seven. It only had two things on it—the photo from the postcard, and four lines of text that Mom and I knew by heart. The minute we drove past the *Welcome to Eagle Waters* sign, we put on our best radio-announcer voices and traded lines.

"THE SPECTACULAR SHOWBOAT RESORT: Where True Blue Friends Meet!"

"EXPERIENCE the pine air—a TREAT for your lungs!"

"The resort of your DREAMS—AWAY from the modern world!"

A glimpse of blue water glistened between the trees on the left side of the highway.

"That's Thunder Lake!" Mom said. Her eyes sparkled like Christmas Eve.

We shouted the last line with gusto as we drove past a yellow church, a gas station, and a small blue house with a sign that read *Anna Lee's Little Store.*

"Don't DELAY! Call TODAY: 555-SHO-BOAT!"

Mom pointed across the street from Anna Lee's. "There's the public beach. If they still give free swim lessons, I'll sign you up."

"That's a beach?" It was an empty patch of sand the length of a school bus.

And then the trees closed in again. The branches got thicker and closer together until we couldn't see Thunder Lake on the side of the road anymore.

"Where's the rest of town?"

"That's all," Mom said. "Quaint, right?"

A pang of disappointment poked at me, but I pushed it away. There'd be so much to do at the resort, we'd never need to go to town.

After another mile, the GPS beeped. On the left side of the road, a wooden arrow with black hand-painted letters announced: *THE SHOWBOAT RESORT.*

Mom put on her blinker and winked at me.

"I forgot to tell you," she said. "Remember Maddy Quinn? Mary Pepper's daughter from Chicago? You two used to . . ."

She turned the Beemobile onto a gravel road and the rumble of rocks under the wheels drowned out her voice, but I knew exactly who she was talking about. I didn't remember much about Chicago, but I remembered Maddy Quinn. We used to make forts out of pillows and hide while Gramps pretended to be a fire-breathing dragon.

Another sign led us onto a dirt path so narrow that pine branches scraped the sides of our car. Mom shouted over the din like it was perfectly normal to drive straight into the heart of a forest. "I heard the Quinns still spend summers in Eagle Waters. Think she'll remember you?"

"Maybe," I said. "It was a long time ago."

It *was* a long time ago, but the thought of the Quinns at The Showboat made my brain buzz with hopeful possibilities. Since Chicago, Mom and I had moved nine times. I'd used up boxes of stationery writing to girls I'd known, and not a single one wrote back. But I'd never moved to a town where somebody knew me.

We made another turn, and Mom had to slow to a snail's pace to avoid ripping the bottom off the car.

"Gillis Girls Don't Believe in Maybe. If she doesn't remember you, remind her!"

She had a point. Quickly, I reached into my backpack and pulled out my notebook, turning to a dog-eared page in the center:

TRUE BLUE FRIEND CRITERIA
1. Shares secrets
2. Keeps promises
3. Likes the same things you like
4. Would rather be with you than anyone else
5. Makes you laugh until your stomach hurts
6. Shows up when needed
7. Is loyal to the bitter end

I added a new line to the list:

8. Remembers you when you move away

The bumpy road made my handwriting all jiggly until suddenly, Mom stopped the car. My pencil jerked, dragging the tail of the "y" right off the page. I looked up. The road had split again, but there was no arrow to guide us. Thunder Lake was nowhere in sight. The voice on the GPS said, "Recalculating . . ." and Mom's phone started to blink a new message: *No Service.*

Mom laughed. "Away from the modern world—as advertised!"

We got out of the car and Mom made wide, sweeping circles with her phone, looking for a signal. The website was right—the air smelled exactly like the pine-scented potpourri Mom always kept in the bathroom.

"I forgot about mosquitoes." Mom swatted her hands in the air.

It was only four in the afternoon, but in the woods, it felt like twilight. Branches filtered the sunlight so only small patches of ground were lit up. When I imagined The Showboat Resort, I never pictured trees. Mom's stories were about waterskiing and sunbathing. Not wilderness survival. I glanced around to make sure there weren't any wild animals waiting to pounce.

Something rustled in the trees. I stiffened and tugged Mom's sleeve. Near a scrubby trio of baby pines, a crouched figure crept in slow motion away from us.

"Hello?" Mom called.

The figure froze, one leg suspended in the air. It was a boy. With branches sprouting from his limbs.

"We're trying to find The Showboat Resort."

"We can see you," I added. A mosquito bit through my sweatshirt and I slapped at it.

The boy let his leg drop to the ground, then shifted some of the branches around and crouched lower. "How about now?" he asked. "Can you see me now?"

The bugs must have caught a whiff of Mom's Honeycomb Highlighting Shampoo. A full-on swarm formed around her head.

"We need to know the way to The Showboat," she said, hopping from foot to foot.

The boy trudged toward us, yanking branches out of

his T-shirt collar. As he got closer, I could see mud caked to his hair, his right arm, and his face. His left arm was in a cast.

"Camouflage never works," he said sadly.

I stared at him. Either there was something in the woods scary enough to hide from, or testing camouflage was a thing kids in Eagle Waters did for fun.

The boy walked a slow circle around the Beemobile. Mom was already back in the driver's seat with the windows rolled up tight.

"Cool car!"

"We're getting eaten alive!" Mom shouted through the glass.

The boy pulled one last pine branch out of the waistband of his pants and waved it in the direction we'd come from. "Turn right at the fork, but . . ." He wrinkled his dirt-caked nose in my direction. "Why would you want to go to The Showboat?"

"We're staying there," I said.

"Like, overnight?"

"Of course." This kid was bizarre. What else would you do at a resort?

I got in the car, and the boy watched us back up the whole way to the fork. He stood covered in mud, with sticks and leaves in his hair, and waved his branch at us with a goofy look on his face. Like he thought *we* were the ones who were strange.

3

THE SPECTACULAR
SHOWBOAT RESORT

In some ways, The Showboat looked exactly like the postcard. The building was boat-shaped. It had round windows, a black smokestack, and a blue lake that sparkled behind it.

But there were no daisies in the field, only tall weeds and dandelions.

The paint on the hotel was dull and peeling—more dirt-gray than white—and two of the grimy porthole windows were cracked.

Instead of a smiling girl waving from the deck, there was a sign hanging from a broken railing: *DO NOT ENTER—Upper Deck Temporarily Closed for Repairs.* Except the sign looked old and faded, too, like there was nothing "temporary" about it.

A red light over the front door blinked on and off: *Vacancy*. No kidding—the only thing in the parking lot besides the Beemobile was a rusty basketball hoop with no net.

All the hope and tingly excitement I'd felt on the drive disappeared like the air in a popped balloon. Mom stared straight ahead, recalculating. I knew she was running through the possible options—throwing out the bad ideas, categorizing the potentially good ones and analyzing them for flaws. I knew we'd sit in the Beemobile until she could come up with a new plan that would be as good, if not better, than the first.

Except the longer we sat, the thicker the silence got. Mom wasn't offering any options.

"Is there another hotel?" I asked.

Mom shook her head. "We can't get the deposit back. I already called and asked."

"You did?" That was news to me. "Why?"

Just then, a light went on in the big bay window of the hotel. Someone pretended to fuss with the curtains—probably wondering what kind of creepy people lurk around a deserted parking lot in a car that looks like a bee.

The shadow behind the curtain was short and appeared to be wearing a long dress. From her height, I guessed she was my age or younger. She disappeared, and seconds later, the bottom of the curtain started to lift. A pair of binoculars appeared on the windowsill, and the shadow crouched behind them, peering at us like a spy.

I didn't know what else to do. I waved.

The shadow shot straight up. Then the girl reached her hand under the curtain and waved back a wiggly-finger wave. Something about it made me breathe easier. Maddy Quinn used to wave like that, each finger dancing individually in the air. She used to wave at me when we were in Silent Time-Out—which happened a lot when Gramps pretended to storm the castle. Every time he roared his dragon roar, we'd get so scared and worked up that one of us would scream, and for some reason, that always made us laugh. We'd laugh and scream until our stomachs hurt, and Mom would have to make us go to Time-Out so we could calm down.

It would be nice. Having a friend like that again.

I thought it over. Things always turned out best when Mom and I had a goal and stuck to the plan. In Milwau-kee, Mom had the worst sales quarter of her life. She could have cried her eyes out and given up, but she didn't. She stayed positive. She stuck to the plan. If she hadn't, we'd be celebrating the last day of fifth grade eating beans and rice in our tiny apartment and arguing with Mr. Li about rent. Instead, we were at The Showboat Resort. It didn't matter if it was beautiful. It mattered that we were here.

"Mom," I whispered, but she was either still thinking or she'd been telepathically frozen by a mutant with psionic powers like Emma Frost. She never took this long to recalculate.

I reached for the glove box and took out a stick of Honey Blossom Bee-You-tiful Lipstick.

"It might be nicer on the inside," I said. "And we can still make s'mores." I put the lipstick in Mom's hand and gave her the best can-do smile I had in me. "Gillis Girls Always Stick to the Plan, right?"

Mom studied the lipstick, turning it over in her hand. She looked at me. She looked at the beaten-down hotel. Then, slowly, she uncapped the tube and pulled the rearview mirror toward herself. She applied a thick, rosy layer, and smacked her lips.

"This place could use some sprucing up," she said. Like all it needed was a good volumizing shampoo and a set of organic loofahs. "But I've seen worse. You're right, Anthoni. Positive Thoughts Attract Positive Results. Let's go check in."

Yes. Positive thoughts. I opened my door and let the pine air swallow me whole.

4

THE BLUE HERON

The door marked *Front Office* creaked on its hinges and shut behind us, sucking up every last bit of outside light with it. At first, I thought I saw two women standing in front of a wall of books, but as my eyes adjusted to the dim light, I realized that one of the women was a lamp—a life-size statue of a mermaid holding a light bulb and a pink shade over her head.

An elderly woman with bright-orange hair stood next to the lamp, waiting in the glow. She wore a silver evening gown covered with butterflies—the kind of dress a movie star might wear if they had the Academy Awards when Abraham Lincoln was alive. The gown shushed as she stepped toward the "front desk," which was actually a stacked-up set of old-fashioned traveling trunks plastered with stickers that read *Chicago: The Palace*, *New York: Hippodrome Theatre*, and *San Francisco: Orpheum Opera House*. Around us, the walls were covered with framed newspapers, black-and-white photos, and posters advertising strange things like *MASTER HOMER, CHAMPION BOY WHISTLER* and *UPSIDE-DOWN STANLEY, THE TOPSY-TURVY FELLOW*.

The room felt like a forgotten museum, not a hotel.

"Are you the person I talked with on the phone?" Mom asked. "I know you said the deposit is nonrefundable, but I was wondering if special circumstances might . . ."

Special circumstances? I thought Mom had said "positive thoughts." Special circumstances sounded like leaving.

Silently, the woman handed Mom a form that had *Carrie & Anthoni Gillis: Six Weeks, Paid in Full* written at the top in swirly pink script. She stabbed a bony finger at a line that read *All Deposits Are Nonrefundable. No Exceptions*.

Mom shook it off with a smile. She put on her chirpy Chief Pollinator voice and said, "I'm *so* glad to be back at The Showboat Resort. I always felt like magical, impossible things could happen here."

I relaxed a little. Mom was back on track. Mostly. But her voice was a notch too cheerful.

"Do they still have swimming lessons in town?

Anthoni's never been here before, and if she can get the basics, we could have Mr. Boulay get her up on water skis . . ."

At the mention of Mr. Boulay, the woman shook her head, dangly butterfly earrings swinging from her lobes.

"Oh, he didn't . . . He's not . . . *gone*, is he?"

A slow, steady, flame-orange head nod.

Mom stopped talking, and an awkward silence filled the room.

"Have the Quinns checked in?" I asked. "I saw a girl in the window."

The butterfly woman gave me a confused look. I realized she hadn't said a single word yet.

I tried again. "She waved at me. Behind the curtain."

The woman smiled, revealing a smudge of lipstick on a crooked front tooth. She shook her shoulders like she'd heard a good joke, then lifted her hand into a wiggly-finger wave.

The girl behind the curtain wasn't a girl at all. She was a very short old woman in a party dress with lipstick on her tooth. *Happy thoughts*, I reminded myself. *Focus on the positive.*

Mom put her hand on my back. "It's only the middle of June. Maddy's school might not be out yet." She turned to the woman behind the desk. "Could you please tell us when Mary Pepper is checking in?"

The woman didn't respond.

"Mary *Pepper*," Mom repeated with an edge of irritation. She caught herself and added in a friendlier voice, "Mary and I became True Blue Friends at this very resort. Life comes full circle, doesn't it?"

The woman flipped through a calendar without looking. Then she opened her mouth and spoke for the first time. Her voice was flat.

"No Pepper."

Mom didn't flinch. "Of course. She *used* to be Pepper. You must have her down as Mary Quinn."

This time, the woman didn't even check. "No Quinn."

Mom bit her lip, then handed over the completed form and beamed like we'd checked into the Taj Mahal.

"We're *so excited* to be here at your beautiful resort!" she said, even chirpier than the first time. She reached into her purse and pulled out a Beauty & the Bee brochure. "We're having a special on the Honey Bee Wrinkle-Free product line for the entire month of June!"

I nudged Mom's foot. I knew selling B&B was a natural reflex for her, but this woman was older than the sun. A whole gallon of unicorn tears wasn't going to help with her wrinkles.

The woman studied the before-and-after pictures of a wrinkle-free woman on the center spread. She let her eyes float dramatically to the ceiling like an actor on a stage. Then, without warning, she shouted, "An elixir of youth!"

I was so surprised that I flinched, and a nervous laugh threatened to burst out of my throat. I choked it down.

"My dear departed grandfather was once a master of the humbug." The woman waved Mom's brochure at a poster on the wall behind her.

DOCTOR HERACLITUS BARNABUS BOULAY
VENTRILOQUIST, MEDICINE MAN,
AND TRICK BICYCLIST
ONE NIGHT ONLY (AT POPULAR PRICES!)

Mom flushed. "That's not at all the same . . ."

The woman slapped the brochure down on the desk and stepped onto a stool. She reached her pale arm to a row of keys, and chose one attached to a wooden carving of a skinny bird with a long beak.

"You've been upgraded," she said. "The Blue Heron: your *own* lakeside cabin."

"We're not going to be in the hotel?" Mom sounded disappointed, but I felt relieved. We'd be fine on our own. Better, even.

"The great blue heron is an extremely self-reliant creature," the woman said. "Surprisingly adaptable to change."

The butterfly dress crinkled as she bunny-hopped off the stool.

"Herons," she announced, "have also been known to choke to death. Trying to swallow fish too big for their skinny throats!"

She leaned over the counter toward me, stretched out her neck, and sucked in her cheeks so hard her face hollowed and her jawbone jutted out beneath her skin. Her eyes bugged like they were going to pop out of her head and roll around on the floor.

Mom froze in place, smile and all, and I started to worry. Was the old woman sick? Was she going to keel over and die right there at the front desk? There probably wasn't a hospital around for miles.

Then she winked at me and began to gulp. She gulped and gulped at the air like a panicky heron with butterfly barrettes who'd swallowed a fish too big for her throat.

Mom gasped, but I couldn't help it—I started to laugh. I tried to hold it in, but the harder I tried, the more giggles bubbled up and flowed out like too much soap in the dishwasher.

The woman paused mid-swallow and studied me, surprised. "You like that?" she asked.

I hiccupped helplessly through my giggles, and the orange-haired woman grinned, showing off the lipstick on her tooth again. She slapped her hand on the desk and chucked a fist under her chin.

"I got a million of 'em," she said in a new, wisecracking voice. "Ask me to do Bear-in-a-Beehive. That one kills 'em every time."

Mom put her purse on her shoulder and tugged on my arm. "I think we're all set," she said. "Thank you very much, Mrs. . . ."

"Boulay. Charlotte Boulay atch'r service."

5

IMPOSSIBLE THINGS

It was a shriek that woke me the first time.

I tugged the sheet close to my face and lay still as a statue, my heart pounding and my eyes fixed on a tall, lean shadow draped across my bed. Each time I breathed, the shadow swayed.

"Mom?" I whispered.

I scanned the loft of The Blue Heron. There was no bear behind the dresser. No woodsman with an axe climbing the ladder from the living room. I propped myself up on my elbow and slowly turned to look at the window seat tucked under the eaves next to my bed.

The cushioned seat glowed in the moonlight—empty. I relaxed. It was only the moon shining through the window, throwing the shadow of a pine tree across my bed. Probably the shriek had been a dream.

Wide-awake, I wrapped myself in a blanket and climbed onto the window seat. I was glad my window faced the lake and not the woods. The Showboat Resort had eight private cabins—all named after animals—built in a semicircle around the main hotel. But while the main building was set in the middle of the open, weed-filled clearing, all of the cabins were hidden along the field's edges in what seemed like the deepest, darkest part of the forest. A curved path that could have been a set piece for *Hansel and Gretel* connected The Red Fox to The Whitetail to The Osprey and eventually wound down toward the water.

The Black Bear and The Blue Heron were the two cabins farthest from the main building and closest to the water. Between them, the path led to a wide set of stairs that looked like bleachers. From my window seat, I could see a dilapidated dock at the bottom of the stairs, stretching out over Thunder Lake. The lake was the shape of a lopsided jelly bean, and larger than I'd expected, but The Showboat was tucked into a small, isolated crook of the bay. In the dark, the trees on the shoreline made a wall of shadow, penning in the cabins, the bleachers, and the moonlit dock.

A breeze rustled in through the screen. I shivered. There was something odd about the resort. Something stranger than run-down cabins and an empty parking lot. It was like Mom said. A *feeling*. Like impossible things could happen. Mom seemed to think that was a good thing, but I wasn't sure.

The shriek came again.

Ooo-OO-oooo

The howling rang across the lake like a woman wailing. Was someone hurt? Was a wild animal out on the hunt? For a brief minute, I let myself wonder if werewolves were a real thing. I thought about going down to the back bedroom and climbing into bed with Mom, but I knew what she would say. Change Your State. Negative Thoughts Attract Negative Results.

I tried to pull the window shut, but it stuck. Everything in The Blue Heron seemed to have a malfunction. The kitchen counter was chipped and coffee-stained, the cushions on the wicker furniture sagged, and the pipes made clunking noises when you turned on the water. So far, the loft was the only thing that wasn't disappointing— the walls slanted up toward the ceiling, and from the foot of the bed you could see down to the kitchen and living room. It was like a cozy tree house you could sleep in. Except for the shrieking.

One more time, I thought. *If I hear it one more time, I'll go get Mom.*

I drew the blanket closer around my shoulders, leaned my back against the wall, and tried to stay vigilant.

* * *

It was a splash that woke me the second time. Loud, like a boulder crashing through the water's surface. I jerked awake and almost fell off the window seat.

In the early morning light, the lake water rippled in large circles in front of the dock like something big had fallen, jumped, or been thrown into Thunder Lake right below my window. The circle of ripples grew larger and larger, then faded away, and the lake returned to glass.

"It was a loon," Mom said at breakfast. "They're like ducks, but they call each other in the night."

"It didn't sound like a duck. It sounded like a human. Or a banshee."

"Like this?" She put her hand under her chin, and made a high-pitched *ooo-OO-oooo* sound in the back of her throat.

"How'd you do that?"

"Loon call."

I didn't think she would make it up or steer me wrong. But it didn't seem right. Birds shouldn't make shrieking sounds in the middle of the night.

"We'll get you some earplugs. You'll sleep like a log."

"Maybe," I said.

6

POTENTIALS

I hope you guys don't need any live bait. It's super icky, and my mom had to run next door, so I'm holding the counter for her. But I can help you with anything. Except bait. Unless you really need it."

The girl on the stool behind the counter of Anna Lee's Little Store was small enough to be a third grader, but she wore glittery eye shadow that matched her lime-green Waterbugs Water-Ski Club T-shirt, and she was painting her nails with a putrid-smelling lime-green polish. Her fingers were splayed out on a giant glass-topped cooler, like the kind that regular convenience stores use to hold ice-cream bars and popsicles, but this one had a sign advertising *NIGHT CRAWLERS, LEECHES, FATHEADS, and SUCKERS—FRESHEST IN TOWN!*

"How about earplugs?" Mom asked, and the girl breathed a sigh of relief. She capped the polish and blew on her nails.

"Those are in the back, by the aspirin and toothpaste. I haven't seen you guys before. Where are you from? My name is Julie. I'm eleven and a half, but I'll be twelve in October, so that's practically three-quarters."

"Anthoni's eleven, too! You girls should chat." Mom jabbed me with her elbow and gave me one of her seize-the-day nods. "*F.E.T.s*," she whispered. Then she turned on her heel and left me alone with Julie and the night crawlers.

F.E.T.s were Beauty & the Bee's First Encounter Tactics. They were easy-to-remember things like "Introduce Yourself," "Share a Personal Story," and "Find Something in Common" to help a first meeting get off on the right foot.

Julie grinned at me, revealing a mouthful of braces with lime-green bands. "I always thought Anthoni was a boy's name," she said, "but it's nice. I once knew a girl named Sam, but it was short for Samantha. You could go by something short. Ann, or Toni? How about Annie?"

"Just Anthoni," I said. "It's my grandpa's name."

Julie scrunched her eyebrows, clearly waiting for more information.

"My mom thought I was going to be a boy, and she always sticks with the plan," I said.

"That's funny. What about initials? The new boy in our class is named Dana, which is kind of like a girl's name, but he goes by DJ. He's an odd duck, though. Not that I think *you* are or anything." She picked up the polish. "Want me to do your nails? It glows in the dark, but don't wear it around my guinea pig, Lavender. It freaks her out."

I looked around the store for something else to talk about. I didn't want to hurt her feelings, but I hate the smell of nail polish and guinea pigs creep me out. I spotted some Archie comics on a rack with postcards.

"Do you have any X-Men?"

"Oh my gosh." Julie huffed like I'd brought up a touchy subject. "My best friend is obsessed and I can't figure out why. Who wants to read about mutates fighting and blowing each other up all the time?"

"Mutants," I said. "The Fantastic Four are mutates. Not X-Men."

Julie scrunched up her nose. She was the only living, breathing person my age I'd seen in Eagle Waters, so I *had* to put her on my Potential Friends list, but we weren't exactly scoring points on the compatibility test.

"Either way. Yuck. My parents would never put violent comics in the store. We like things to be super wholesome, you know? Is this your first time here? Are you going to join the ski team? You should. The varsity boys are *so* cute this year. Where are you guys staying?"

Julie paused long enough for me to say, "The Show-boat," and then she sucked air through her braces.

"Really? That's not, uhhhh . . ." She turned her head toward the window. "Hey! Is your car shaped like a bee?"

She hopped down from her stool to get a better look. "It is! It looks exactly like a bee! That is so cool! Can I take a picture? I've got to take a picture!"

While Julie fiddled with her phone, trying to find the best angle through the window, I found Mom in the toothpaste/cat food/peanut butter aisle.

"She's nice," Mom whispered. "But more of a Connector than a Potential?"

I nodded. One good way to build a Potentials list is to meet a Connector and get introduced to all their friends.

The store door jingled and a peal of laughter filled the room.

"Julie, *don't* tell me your mother bought that hideous car! What are you running here—a circus?"

I turned around to glare at the rude woman, but Mom took one look at her, grabbed my arm, and dragged me to the farthest aisle. We squatted in front of a shelf full of baby food.

"What are you doing?" I whispered, trying to wrestle out of her grip.

Mom picked up a jar of mashed beets. "Pretend like we're talking."

"We *are* talking. Why are we squatting? Are you feeling okay?"

"Mrs. Quinn!" Julie squealed. "It's not our car, it's my friend Anthoni's. Is Maddy here?"

The door jingled again and Julie let out another ear-piercing squeal. "MADDEEEEEEEEE!"

Maddy? Maddy *Quinn*? I peered around the aisle and caught a glimpse of navy-blue high-tops.

Mom's face was white, which didn't make sense. If that was Maddy Quinn, then the woman must be Mary Pepper. The same Mary Pepper who swam with Mom in "magical" Thunder Lake six summers in a row. Why were we pretending to talk about baby food?

Julie appeared in the aisle behind us, holding her wet nails in front of herself like a TV doctor getting ready to perform surgery. When I saw the girl standing next to her, I couldn't keep the grin off my face. Maddy Quinn didn't look at all like the girl in pigtails I remembered, but she had a rolled-up comic book in her hand. I couldn't exactly tell what it was, but I saw the Marvel logo and a sliver of what looked like a metal claw.

"Oh, thank goodness!" Julie said. "I thought they disappeared, and that would have been so weird. I've never had anyone disappear in the store before. This is my new friend, Anthoni. She's the one with the bee car."

"Carrie Gillis?" Mrs. Quinn said. "I haven't seen you

since the girls were in kindergarten. What on *earth* are you doing here?"

Mom stood and chitchatted with Mrs. Quinn like she would with any stranger she met on the street. Why weren't they jumping up and down and hugging like True Blue Friends who hadn't seen each other in years? I swallowed a few butterflies and gave Maddy a friendly wave. She jutted her chin toward me in a nod and bent her head close to Julie's.

"I used to know her," she said. It was barely audible, but I heard it. Maddy Quinn remembered me.

"Have you seen The Showboat?" Mrs. Quinn asked. "You won't even recognize it. It's gone downhill ever since Mr. Boulay's daughter took over."

"Charlotte?" I asked.

Mrs. Quinn looked surprised. "You know her?"

"Anthoni's staying there," Julie said.

Maddy make a choking sound. "Seriously?"

"Where are *you* staying?" I asked.

Mrs. Quinn gave me the kind of smile you give to a five-year-old who's said something cute.

"Leon and I bought a log cabin after I got promoted to partner at the firm," she told Mom. "But then we decided to get out of the rat race and move here year-round. Quality of life is more important than working yourself into the ground, don't you think?" She reached out and touched Mom's elbow. "I can't believe you didn't know that, Carrie. It's been too long!"

Maddy whispered something to Julie, and as she turned, she tucked the rolled-up comic into her back pocket. It unrolled enough so I could see what it was. *Wolverine and the X-Men.*

Mrs. Quinn slapped her hands together. "Cancel your reservation. You and Anthoni are going to stay with us."

I couldn't believe it. In a matter of seconds, we'd gone from a dumpy old resort to staying at a log cabin with someone who was going to become my True Blue Friend. I could *feel* it. It was in my head, clear as day—Maddy Quinn and I sharing a room, trading comics, telling secrets, and making each other laugh until our sides hurt.

"Oh no," Mom said. "We love The Showboat. It's perfect."

"You do?" Julie asked.

I had to pick my jaw up off the floor. *Perfect? Love?*

Mrs. Quinn sounded almost relieved. "At least come for dinner, then. How about next week . . ." Her voice trailed off as she noticed the baby-food beets in Mom's hand. "Another baby? Carrie, I didn't know!"

Mom straightened herself up to her full height and smiled her super-confident B&B smile. "Oh, this?" she said, holding out the beets. "These are great for smoothies. The antioxidants do wonders for your skin tone. You should try it."

Julie sidled up to me and started to giggle. "You hear something new every day," she said. "Baby-food smoothies. *Beet* baby-food smoothies! It's pretty weird, but I'd try it. Wouldn't you, Maddy?"

Maddy Quinn chewed a fingernail and looked me over like she was sizing me up along with the beets.

"I don't think so," she said.

For a split second, the dark tone in her voice squashed the floating-on-clouds feeling I'd had since she walked into the store. But another glance at the Wolverine comic convinced me I was on the right track. *Maybe* . . . I thought, and then I caught myself. Gillis Girls Don't Believe in Maybe. I had hard work and stick-to-itiveness on my side. All I needed was a plan.

7

QUEEN BEE

On our way home from Anna Lee's, it started to sprinkle, and by the time we got to The Blue Heron, rain was pelting down. It churned up the surface of Thunder Lake until the water was gray and choppy. Mom had wanted to spend our first day swimming, but instead, we split up the items on our Gillis Girls Clean Team checklist. We scrubbed every inch of the avocado-green refrigerator and vacuumed the red-and-white-checked curtains.

The cabin was small, so it didn't take long. The kitchen was only a sink, a stove, and a picnic table in a corner of the living room. There was a tiny bathroom, Mom's bedroom, and the loft. When every task had been completed, the air smelled like Organic Grapefruit Cleanser instead of dust, and The Blue Heron felt less disappointing than it had the night before.

Mom hung her whiteboard above the picnic table while I made some ramen for lunch. I grabbed a couple issues of *Wolverine and the X-Men* and collapsed into one of the chairs next to the wicker couch.

"You didn't tell me about these," I said.

The Blue Heron might not have much going for it, but it had two incredibly cool chairs. They were made out of rope and hung suspended from the ceiling, like hammocks, only better. Each chair was a cozy, swinging hive full of pillows. At first, I worried the one I'd sat down in would collapse, sending me, my soup, and the comics tumbling onto the floor. But surprisingly, it held.

Mom finished drawing a Potential Clients column on her whiteboard, then sat in the chair next to me and used her feet to sway back and forth while she slurped her noodles. She looked like she'd slept less than I had.

"This place used to be really popular," she said. "When Gram and Gramps were kids, movie stars came here all the time. Bob Hope stayed every summer."

"Who's Bob Hope?"

Mom sighed. "Exactly," she said. "It's not the same world anymore."

We sat for a while, swinging and slurping while I read

and Mom looked out at Thunder Lake. The rain had stopped and a bright, happy blue was taking over the sky. The bottoms of the clouds were still dark, but the sun's rays sparkled on the lake like spilled glitter.

"Magic," Mom breathed.

I flipped through a comic with Jean Grey's School for Higher Learning on the cover. Talk about magic. Mutant kids are always meeting each other at that school and becoming friends for life. No matter what happens after they leave—if they lose their family, or even if they lose their powers—they stay friends. They stick up for each other, make jokes together, and always show up when needed. I'd been to nine schools, and I'd never found a friend like that. But Maddy . . .

"Hey, Mom, do you still have last year's issues of *Buzz from the Hive*?"

"Sure, why?"

"Just . . . I remembered an article I want to read again."

"They're in my 'Collateral' box in the bedroom," she said.

I retrieved the stack of newsletters and spread them on the picnic table in the kitchen. I sorted through articles like "How to Build a Buzzing Potentials List" and "Five First-Encounter Tactics to Help You Sweeten the Pot." The article I was looking for was in last year's June issue on page two:

How to Discover Your Client's Secret Dream
and Become the Person Who
Can Make That Dream Come True
By Carrie Gillis

*You'll no longer have a client, you'll have a
True Blue Friend for life—guaranteed!*

ACTION STEPS:
1. Meet Potential Clients
   ☐ Join an activity
2. Narrow In
   ☐ Identify your best Potential and Make
   a Meaningful Connection
3. Develop Trust
   ☐ Don't bee needy; find a way to bee needed
4. Discover Her Secret Dream
   ☐ Bee a careful listener
5. Do What It Takes
   ☐ Become the person who can make that
   dream come true!

I remembered helping Mom with the list. I'd even come up with the "bee" puns, which I'd been pretty proud of. At the time, we were only trying to fill space in the newsletter, but now, the Action Steps looked like points plotted on a treasure map.

I grabbed my notebook and turned to a blank page. In block letters, I wrote *TRUE BLUE FRIEND: ACTION STEPS* and copied down Mom's list. I could already check off number one, *Join an activity*. There'd been a swim lesson sign-up sheet at Anna Lee's, and while Mom filled it out, Julie had cheered her on: "Yay! *Everyone's* going to be there! Fun!"

Everyone, I assumed, included Maddy Quinn.

As I wrote down number two, *Narrow In: Identify your Best Potential*, I grinned. Maddy was easily the Best Potential I'd ever had. Like the kids at Jean Grey's School for Higher Learning, we shared a backstory. She'd liked me once. We'd fought dragons together.

Next to number two, I penciled in *Maddy Quinn* and drew stars around the name. Making a plan felt great. Ever since Mom had mentioned Maddy, I'd felt like the universe was shouting at me: *Now. Now is your chance.* It was my job to take charge and make it happen. Like Mom did with Queen Bee. Like she always did. With everything.

By the time I put down my pencil, Mom was back at her whiteboard making her own list. Under her Potential Clients column, she'd written the words "Charlotte Boulay" and added three Action Steps under her name:

1. Free Sample
2. Bee-You-tiful Makeover
3. Home Party

"Charlotte Boulay?" I asked. "Really?"

"Mr. Boulay used to tell our ski team about his daughter who worked in Hollywood with all these famous movie stars. It has to be her, don't you think?"

"Probably. So?"

"Don't you think she'd have good connections?"

I wrinkled my nose. "I don't know . . ."

"Even if she doesn't, Charlotte would be an ideal Worker Bee," Mom said. "She could sell Golden Nectar Sunscreen in the front office."

Out of nowhere, I felt a flash of annoyance.

"To who? Loons?"

Mom winced.

I felt bad. I didn't know why I'd snapped at her. I'd been feeling great a second ago, but now my chest felt tight.

"Sorry," I said.

"I know what you mean. But tourist season doesn't kick off until the Fourth of July. The Showboat will be hopping with people by then."

She added "Target Date: July 4" next to Charlotte Boulay's name, but she wrote the words slowly, like she didn't believe them, and she added a question mark at the end.

I realized what was bothering me.

"Why are you working?" I asked.

"Why wouldn't I be?"

47

"Um . . . we're on vacation?" I said. "Besides, you're Queen Bee now. Recruiting Worker Bees is the Pollinator's job."

Mom set her marker down.

"We should talk about that."

She scratched a mosquito bite on her wrist before looking me in the eye. Something wasn't right. Had Beauty & the Bee changed the rules? Were they going to give her recruiting duties even though she was a Queen Bee? That wouldn't be fair.

"I'm not Queen Bee, Anthoni," she said quietly. "I didn't make my goal."

It felt like a sucker punch. Like Emma Frost showed up in her diamond form and gave me a swift kick to the jaw.

"Yes, you did," I said. "You told me you did." She wasn't making sense.

"I didn't mean to. You jumped to the conclusion, and you were so happy. I couldn't stand to let you down."

"You *lied* to me?"

It didn't seem possible. I replayed the last two days in my mind, picking apart moments, scenes, all the little things she'd done and said that made me think she was Queen Bee. She'd let me spend two whole days believing that our hard work had paid off. That our ship had come in. She'd let me believe we were done moving from state to state, spending nights and weekends

48

counting inventory and stuffing Healthy Honey Glow sample packs. That we were done bringing our calculator to the grocery store to make sure homemade pizza supplies didn't bust our food budget for the month.

Mom walked over to the window and gazed out at Thunder Lake.

"Then what are we doing here?" I asked. If we hadn't made our goal, we hadn't earned our incentive either. "Tell me the truth."

She sat down on the picnic bench across from me.

"I didn't know what else to do," she said. "Mr. Li needed the rent, and I . . . needed time. To get us back on track."

The words sunk in—*back on track*—and that's when I knew.

Recently, Mr. Li, our landlord, had been stopping by and leaving notes. "Just checking in," he'd say in a sweet voice when I answered the door. I thought he'd turned over a new leaf, acting nice to his tenants, but he was kicking us out.

I felt queasy.

"Did we . . ." I couldn't even think of the right word. Run away? Skip town? Steal?

"I'll send him the rent," Mom said. "I promise. When I couldn't get the Showboat deposit back, I did a cost-benefit analysis, and I thought . . ."

"We'd hide here for six weeks." I looked away from

her. The spectacular Showboat Resort wasn't a disappointment. It was a disaster.

"We're not hiding." Mom sat up straighter and put on a smile. "We're on a detour. Detours can be good. Sometimes they're even Meant to Be . . ."

We sat in silence while Mom stared out at the lake, chewing her lip and thinking. The clouds had disappeared and the whole sky was a brilliant, bright blue. I glared at the sunshine. It felt wrong and out of place.

Worries began to dogpile on top of me: What if we couldn't pay back the rent? Would someone come after us? Mr. Li? The police? What was going to happen in six weeks when our time was up at The Showboat? Where would we go? Not to Gramps. *Mom* convinced him to move to Shady Rest. We couldn't live there. And if we couldn't pay the rent, did we even have money for other stuff? Like food?

The replay in my mind sped back weeks, then months. All this time, she must have known things were going badly. Why didn't she tell me? She must have been upset and she didn't say a word. The Gillis Girls were supposed to tell each other everything. We didn't have anybody else. If we couldn't trust each other, we were sunk.

Finally, Mom let out a deep breath.

"I've got a new plan," she said.

I leaned forward.

She stood up and erased everything on the white-board. *Good.* If we were going to dig out of this mess, we needed something a whole lot better than Charlotte Boulay.

What she did next stunned me. She picked up the dry-erase marker and tossed it in the trash.

"Here's what we're going to do," she said. "We're going to put on our bathing suits, go down to the lake, and enjoy this beautiful day."

I'd never seen her like this. Stuck. Buying time. Giving up. It seemed impossible that my mom—my unstop-pable, stick-to-itive mom—didn't know what to do. And we were trapped at The Showboat Resort until she could figure it out.

"That's not a plan," I said.

Mom bit her lip. "I know, honey. But right now, it's all I've got."

8

THUNDER LAKE

It was a short walk down the Hansel and Gretel path to the wooden bleachers I'd seen from the loft. The ground was wet under my bare feet and pine needles stuck between my toes. The forest was blanketed in a post-storm damp and hush that managed to feel peaceful and terrifying at the same time.

I'd put on the old Waterbugs Water-Ski Club swimsuit that Mom had saved for two decades in her memory box. It smelled like mothballs, but it fit okay. I felt strange walking half-naked through the woods in a suit borrowed from a person who'd been lying to me for months. I pulled my towel tightly around my shoulders to distract myself from the nervous chill that had settled into my bones.

I'd never been swimming, not even at the YMCA. I'd wanted to, but Mom always said pools were disgusting and when she got to be Queen Bee, I'd learn to swim the right way—in Thunder Lake. Except she wasn't Queen Bee. And we weren't doing *anything* the right way.

Mom tossed me her towel the minute she stepped onto the dock, took two quick strides, and dove into the lake. The rickety dock swayed as if it might collapse, and I sat down to avoid toppling into the water. Rain that had pooled on the wood seeped into my suit, spreading the bone-chill deeper. Any positive thoughts I'd ever had about learning how to swim vanished into thin air. Up close, Thunder Lake, like everything else about The Showboat and possibly my entire life, wasn't nearly as spectacular as I'd imagined.

When you saw it from far away, like in a postcard or from a window seat in a cabin loft, Thunder Lake looked blue. But when you got close enough to put your toes in, it was a sickly color—orange-brown, with weeds and lily pads covering the surface in patches. About two feet offshore, the rusty water turned so deep and dark that you couldn't see through it. I shuddered. It wasn't the green film growing on the surface that bothered me. It was something more sinister. The lake seemed bottomless. Unknowable. Like you could get sucked in and never come out.

When she surfaced, Mom propped her elbows on the dock and kicked her legs out behind her like a kid.

"Put your feet in," she said. "It feels heavenly."

I stared at the spot where her feet kicked the water into a froth—exactly where the eerie ripples had formed and faded early this morning—and I kept my feet where they were.

"Can you see Anna Lee's?" she asked, pointing across Thunder Lake.

Almost directly on the other side of the lake, I could see a rectangular patch of sand that I thought must be the public beach, and behind it, the blue store. In the distance, a speedboat pulling a water-skier zipped past the yellow church, and a sailboat floated near the shore. On our side of the lake, in the bay, the only movement was a family of ducks bobbing along, occasionally tipping their heads into the water and flashing white tails.

"Once, Mary Pepper and I took inner tubes and floated all the way across to get ice cream at Anna Lee's," Mom said. "It took us an hour to get over there and two hours to get back because of the wind. It was the best ice cream I'd ever had!"

Mom pushed her wet bangs out of her face, and a trick of the light made the dark circles under her eyes disappear. I knew she wanted me to smile or laugh. But I couldn't.

"Thunder Lake felt so magical," she continued. "It

seemed like incredible, amazing things were happening all the time."

"Like what?"

I looked around for a spark of magic—something incredible and amazing that would send that Meant to Be tingle down my neck. I didn't need it to be big. I'd take anything that would make this disaster of a summer seem like a detour worth taking. Instead, my eyes settled on a cluster of brown, slimy, half-eaten lily pads.

Mom pushed herself away from the dock. "Like this."

She ducked her head, did a somersault under the water, and emerged laughing. That was the thing about Mom. Even after our entire Five-Year Plan had fallen apart, the Gillis Girls trust had evaporated, and The Showboat Resort had turned out to be a tragic dump, she could find a way to laugh. Mom never waited for magic to come to her. She made her own.

"Watch. Dolphin dive," she said, and leaped out of the water high enough to dive back down, letting her feet flip in the air like a dolphin tail.

It hit me that I'd never seen Mom swim. She was different in the lake—lighter, happier, more like herself. As mad as I was at her, I felt a seed of hope plant itself in my brain. We could fix this. It might not be easy, but if we stayed positive and worked hard, we could create our own destiny. We *had* to. And if Mom couldn't come up with a decent plan, I would.

"Where are we?" I asked. "Number-wise. How many Worker Bees did you sign up at the air-conditioning conference?"

Mom treaded water with her arms. "I didn't go. It wasn't a great idea to begin with. You're not really supposed to sell at a conference unless you're an official sponsor."

She didn't even go. I wanted to grind my teeth, but I shook it off.

"How many do we need? Not to make Queen Bee. Just to pay back Mr. Li."

Mom swam closer and put her elbows back on the dock.

"If we can get five Worker Bees at the Basic level or one at the Premium level before the end of the month, I'll get a bonus that will pay our back rent. But . . . I don't know, Anthoni. That's not much time."

I eyed the murky water. "Swim lessons start Monday, right?"

She nodded.

The last thing I wanted to do was put one toe in that soupy lake, but there were only two weeks left in the month. She needed to meet people.

"Bring your sample kits," I said. "You can pitch the parents on the beach." It was a plan that had worked with my karate class in Cleveland, but there were fifty kids in that class. I didn't know if there were fifty people in the entire town of Eagle Waters.

"I'll . . . try, but . . ."

I forced myself to smile at her. If this was going to work, I knew the number-one thing I had to do was stay upbeat and positive, but "try" was not going to cut it. If anyone should know that, it's Mom. Every Chief Pollinator is trained in the Three Steps to Making It BIG:

1. Bee Positive
2. Invest in Success
3. Get 'er done!

"Difficult Is Just a Challenge," I reminded her.

"Of course. You're right, Anthoni."

Mom let go of the dock and floated on her back, staring up at the clouds with a frown. I practiced my happy thoughts while she backstroked away from me. On Monday, I'd go to swim lessons, and Mom would meet Potential Clients. She'd sign up enough Worker Bees to pay back Mr. Li and then we could start saving for the deposit on our next apartment.

Wherever that would be . . .

I stopped the negative thought before it went any further. Besides, I reminded myself, I had my *own* plan. Everything would be easier once Maddy Quinn and I were True Blue Friends. No matter where I went, she'd write and call. No matter what happened, we'd stay friends. The Showboat was a detour, I decided. The good kind. The Meant to Be kind.

The tightness in my chest loosened, and I felt the seed of hope grow roots. The happy thoughts were working. I tried a few more. The woods weren't scary, they were magical. The nighttime shriek was nothing but a loon. And for all I knew, the splash came from something incredible and amazing like an otter, or a mermaid.

It helped. I felt better. But I still didn't put my feet in the water.

9

SWIM LESSONS

Y ou can let me off here, Mom," I said as soon as
Anna Lee's Little Store came into sight through
the trees. It had taken seven minutes to drive the bumpy
woodland roads leading to the town side of Thunder
Lake, and with every lurch of the Beemobile, I felt more
anxious. The straps of Mom's ancient Waterbugs Water-
Ski Club swimsuit dug into my shoulders like a not-so-
subtle warning. *Danger. Don't go.*

"Don't be silly," Mom said. "I want to meet your
swim teacher."

"You could let me get out while you find parking," I
suggested, but I'd forgotten that Eagle Waters wasn't the
kind of town with parking lots or sidewalks. Eagle
Waters didn't even have a stoplight.

"Too late!" Mom pulled off onto the shoulder of the road, adding the Beemobile to a row of cars lined up on the beach side of the highway. Where had they all come from? There were more people at the beach than Mom and I had seen in three days. I checked to make sure Mom's B&B sample kits were in the bag with the towels.

Mom squeezed my arm. "Rule number one: no swimming without an adult this summer," she said. "Okay?"

I bit the inside of my cheek. "I don't think I want to go in at all," I said.

Mom tsk-ed her tongue and hit me with three of her favorite Mottos for Life. "Negative Thoughts Attract Negative Results. It Doesn't Matter If You Feel Brave; It Matters If You *Act* Brave. Change Your State," she said. "I'll wait."

She tugged at the rearview mirror and opened her tube of Bee-You-tiful Lipstick.

On the other side of the highway, Julie and a little boy wearing bright-yellow arm floaties stood outside Anna Lee's Little Store. She tugged at the boy's arm, trying to get him to cross, but he looked both ways about a thousand times before running top-speed across the pavement to the beach, leaving Julie to race after him.

"See?" Mom said. "Julie's here. You'll make some good connections."

I was *trying* not to be a Negative Nelly, but it was

hard to come up with happy thoughts about swim lessons. It was just a lake. Mom had been swimming in it hundreds of times. But every time I thought about jumping into that murky abyss, my legs got wobbly. What was living down there? What if I jumped in and disappeared without leaving a trace? It was silly, but it didn't help that the way the water in Thunder Lake creeped back and forth on the edge of the sand looked exactly like an evil spirit in a horror movie I once saw. Add that to the shrieking loons and the loud splash that had been waking me up every day at dawn since we'd arrived—there was no way I wanted to get into that lake.

Mom tossed the lipstick into the glove box. "Did you change your state?"

I knew I shouldn't fake it. I should try to think of the whole thing as an exciting challenge and visualize myself swimming until I actually felt happy about it. Instead, I lied. "Sure, it'll be fun."

A group of kids stood on the beach, jumping and pointing at the Beemobile, but when I shut the car door behind me, they scattered toward the lake. The car's antennas bobbed up and down like it was all some hilarious joke.

Compared to the dead-quiet bay at The Showboat, the other side of Thunder Lake was a bustling metropolis. Three Jet Skis zipped around, a guy and a dog sat in a fishing boat, and not too far from the beach, two women in floppy hats stood on wide surfboards and slowly propelled themselves forward with long paddles. The Eagle Waters Community Beach was so small that even though there were only forty or fifty people there, almost every patch of sand was covered with toddlers building sandcastles and parents sitting on towels.

Mom threw her shoulders back in her confident Chief Pollinator pose, and marched me down to meet the swim teacher. Mrs. Nueske was a skinny, overly tanned woman with a Red Cross patch sewn to her swimsuit. She checked my name off a list and blew a silver whistle in the direction of the crowd.

"Class starts in five minutes!" she shouted.

She raised her eyebrows at the giant pink umbrella, folding chair, and beach bag Mom had found in the closet of The Blue Heron. "Good luck finding a place for all that," she said, squeezing her lips shut like she was trying not to laugh. "I always do enjoy it when city people come to visit."

Normally, in a first-day situation, I would check out the scene, make eye contact with a few kids, and introduce myself. But other than the toddlers and a line of junior-high sunbathers in sparkly swimsuits, everyone was already in the water playing a game based entirely on running around and splashing people in the face. I froze until Mrs. Nueske blew three sharp blasts on her whistle. The kids who'd been whooping, hollering, and hurling water at each other gathered in front of us at the edge of the beach. The sparkly-suit girls shook out their towels and clumped together, holding up their arms to compare nonexistent tans.

"DJ!" Mrs. Nueske laid on the whistle. "Sit it out! We're doing buoy drills today, and I don't want to have to save you when that thing weighs you down."

A boy with more freckles than face broke away from the group and trudged back to the beach. He flopped down on the sand and pulled a plastic bag off his arm, revealing a cast. Without mud on his face and branches in his pants, I almost didn't recognize Camo Boy. Was he getting out of swim class because of a broken bone? Ridiculously, I felt jealous. Also, panicked. Buoy drills? Whatever those were, they sounded dangerous. I looked at the Red Cross patch on Mrs. Nueske's suit. How many people had she saved during buoy drills? Was she going to have to save *me*?

Mrs. Nueske blew her whistle and pointed toward the water on one side of the beach. "Tadpoles—left!"

She blew the whistle again. "Minnows—center!"

Thweet! "Muskies—right!"

Thweet! "Junior Lifesavers—CPR station! On the beach!"

Within seconds, everyone scattered. Kids chatted, laughed, and sorted themselves into groups. The sparkly-suit girls giggled their way over to the Junior Lifesavers corner of the beach and the littlest kids splashed their way to a shallow spot toward the left. Julie jumped up and down in waist-high water, waving at me from the Muskies group.

"Anthoni! Hey, Anthoni! Over here!" she shouted.

Maddy Quinn bounced in the water next to her, and I felt a little better. Swim lessons would be worth it if Mom could sign up some Worker Bees and I could accomplish Action Step Two and Make a Meaningful Connection with Maddy. Which shouldn't be hard. All we needed was something in common, and I already knew she liked comics.

I took a deep breath and stepped into the water. Goose bumps popped up on my arms. The water was cold as a freshly melted polar ice cap, yet the other kids were splashing around like it was bathwater. My toes squished into the bottom of the lake. I took another step, and the muck held my foot and sucked it deeper into the slime. I yanked it out and tried to find better footing, but the more I moved my feet, the more they sank.

Was this quicksand? Mom was right. My negative thoughts were attracting negative results. Frantically, I tried to change my state. *This is fun. This is fun. Like stepping in pudding. Fun!* Something slithery and solid squished between my toes and I stopped breathing. *Happy thoughts. Not snakes. Lollipops and rainbows. Not snakes. Not snakes.* Mrs. Nueske blew her whistle in my direction.

"Anthoni Gillis!" she barked. "Hold it right there!"

I made a wish that she'd send me back to the beach like the boy with the cast.

Mrs. Nueske tapped her clipboard in my direction. "Can you butterfly?"

"Excuse me?"

"How's your backstroke?"

Like tennis?

"Can you crawl? Dead Man's Float?"

My swim teacher was from outer space. I was going to drown.

"What grade are you in?" she asked.

"Fifth," I said. "I mean, I just finished. *Sixth*." I couldn't think. The lake water was affecting my brain.

A couple kids tittered, and the teacher shook her head like there wasn't enough pity in the world for a sixth grader who didn't know how to swim.

"Tadpoles!" Mrs. Nueske shouted to the left, where the little kids were picking their noses in the shallow water. "Meet your new teammate: Anthoni Gillis."

10

GILLS

The only thing more embarrassing than getting sent to the kindergartner class when you're eleven years old is getting sent to the kindergartner class and then having to lie in the shallow water and blow bubbles for a half hour while the kids your age swim laps around buoys like they're training for the Olympics.

"Come on, Anthoni. Put your face *in* the water, like Josh is doing," Shari said. Shari was the Tadpole Helper, a teenager with thick layers of purple eyeliner circling her eyes like a raccoon's.

We were lying on our bellies in the shallow, rust-colored water, heads pointing to the beach, feet floating behind us toward the deeper, creepier part of the lake. What we were *supposed* to do was dunk our faces in, blow bubbles for five counts, then lift our heads out and breathe air for five more. I propped myself up on my elbows as far out of the lake as I could get, and each time Shari started counting, I'd dip my head an inch closer and blow on the surface of the water.

It's not like my face had never gotten wet before. I'd dunked my head in the bath hundreds of times—but the water in my bathtub was clear and only went knee-high. It didn't drift off into a bottomless pit two miles wide. I closed my eyes and tried to imagine hot steamy water and bubbles all around. It didn't work. I wasn't going to put my head in Thunder Lake.

Julie's younger brother lay next to me blowing perfect five-count bubbles. He lifted his head out of the lake on count five, gasping for air, water dripping from his hair into his mouth and eyes.

"You could borrow these," he sputtered, pointing to the SpongeBob SquarePants floaties on his arms. "If you want to feel safe."

His swim trunks floated around his skinny legs like a tent. When he came up for air again, he scooted his tiny body closer to me and whispered, "I'm Josh. I used to be scared of the water, too."

"I'm not scared," I said. "I just don't want to put my head in."

He nodded slowly, like an old man who could tell a war story or two. "That's what I used to say."

When Mrs. Nueske blew her whistle and yelled, "Towel up!" I wanted to kiss her. I sprinted out of the water and grabbed my towel and sandals from Mom's bag.

"Watch it, honey! Don't drip on me!"

Mom had her Beauty & the Bee catalog open to the spread that lists 101 Vibrant Shades for Your Inner Queen Bee. She handed a frizzy-haired woman a sample palette and a pocket mirror.

"This shade is really going to make your eyes pop, Eileen," she said, but her voice didn't have her usual Chief Pollinator ring to it. It sounded tired. Bored, even. "See how the orange tones complement those green highlights in your irises?"

The woman blinked into the mirror. "I didn't know my eyes had green in them," she said. "But look at that. You're right!"

I was so cold, my teeth were vibrating and banging together inside my mouth.

"How long do you need?" I asked.

Mom shrugged. "Five more minutes?"

That meant it wasn't going well. If Eileen was hooked, Mom would need at least fifteen minutes to go over the Worker Bee Welcome Packet. I stepped aside and spotted Julie tromping in from the water with a pack of kids from the Muskie group. Josh ran toward them with his arms full of towels, shirts, and sandals. Maddy Quinn ruffled his hair and wrapped herself in a Wolverine towel. At least the morning wouldn't be a total loss.

I put on my sandals and headed in their direction.

Josh waved. "Hi, Anthoni!"

I poked my fingers out from under my towel and wiggled them. *Smile*, I thought. *Look friendly. Take initiative.*

"Anthoni?" A kid in long trunks snorted. "Are you a boy? 'Cause if you are, I gotta warn you—you're wearing a girl's swimsuit."

The rest of the group giggled. I rolled my eyes. Every town I'd lived in had a smart-aleck kid who wanted to show off by picking on the new girl. I knew from experience that the only way to deal with it was to nip it in the bud—instant retaliation. Show one sign of weakness on the first day and it's over.

"Are you a comedian?" I asked. "'Cause if you are, I gotta warn you—you're not funny."

Josh grinned and gave me a thumbs-up.

"Don't be mean, Kurt." Julie swatted the boy with a towel and took a protective stand next to me. "Anthoni was named after her grandfather, and that's a really special thing. Not a lot of girls get to be named after their grandfathers. Besides, Anthoni's my friend. You're not allowed to make fun of her."

Julie tugged my arm free from my towel and linked

her ice-cold elbow through mine. She was so short, she had to stand on her tiptoes a little.

"Kurt's my cousin," she said in a confidential whisper. "You can ignore him."

I shifted uncomfortably. You had to be careful with girls like Julie who want to make sure they're *first* to be friends with the new kid. Once the newness wears off and no one's paying attention anymore, they don't think twice about leaving you in the dust. In Indianapolis, Gracie O'Shay wouldn't let anyone else sit by me for a month and a half, and made sure we were partners in every activity. Then, out of the blue, she told everyone I stole her creepy guinea pig. I had lunch alone a lot that year.

"What's your last name again?" Maddy asked.

"Gillis," I said.

I'd barely said two words, but clearly, something had already gone wrong. Maddy's voice had an edge to it, and she was looking at me like I'd punched her in the stomach. I followed her eyes to Julie's hand on my arm. This was not good. In any new-girl scenario, the only thing worse than a pet-stealer is a friend-stealer. I tried to unlink elbows, but Julie's grip was strong. What was she doing? *Trying* to sabotage my chances with Maddy? My plan to Make a Meaningful Connection didn't account for girls with guinea pigs ruining things from the get-go.

"Gills?" Maddy asked. "See, Kurt, she's not a boy.

70

She's a fish! Must be why she's such a great swimmer. That was some of the best bubble-blowing I've ever seen."

Kurt cracked up and gave Maddy a high-five. I groaned. It doesn't matter where you go—Ohio, Illinois, or an eerie lake in middle-of-nowhere Wisconsin—people come up with the same stale jokes every time. Boy's name. Gills. Like we're all a bunch of robots with the same joke programming. But somehow, it hit harder coming from a girl in an X-Men towel.

Josh crumpled his forehead, confused. "Anthoni didn't blow any bubbles," he said. "She was afraid to put her face in. Like I used to be!"

Julie shushed him, and I took the opportunity to reclaim my arm and tuck it back under my towel. The rest of the group was in hysterics. I glared at Josh, and he shrugged his yellow floaties at me. "Well, it's true," he said.

They whooped it up for a minute before Maddy held out her hands to calm everyone down. "Seriously, guys," she said. She batted her eyelashes and threw me a pouty you-poor-thing look. "I think we should give her a break. Gills has a lot more to be scared of than the water."

"Like what?" I asked, and immediately wished I could take it back. It was a weak response. I should have come up with something that would show Maddy I wasn't the enemy—I was on her team. *I* was the one who would show up when needed and blast the enemy off the page. She just didn't know it yet.

Maddy reached out and laid her hand on my shoulder, making her voice all low and dramatic. "My mom says your mom must need some serious help if you're staying at The Showboat."

I couldn't help it—I started to giggle. Partly because my nerves got the better of me, and partly because the boy with the cast had walked up behind her and was pretending to lick the back of his good hand and wipe it on her hair, like a cat cleaning another cat.

"Hey," she said, "if you're not worried about it, that's cool. But if it was me, I'd watch my back."

The boy took one last good lick and let out a surprisingly realistic "Meow!"

It was so goofy, I burst out laughing, but none of the other kids made a peep. Maddy spun around and slapped at him. "Get away from me, DJ!" she said. "You are such a freak!"

"I guess you should watch *your* back, too," I said with a hopeful smile. I thought a joke might calm everyone down. We could all laugh and start over with a clean slate. It didn't work. Maddy brushed past me, pulling Julie and Kurt behind her.

As the rest of the Muskies scattered, I dug my feet into the sand. The surface was warm from the sun, but inches down, my toes hit a layer of cold, wet mud that sent a shiver up my legs. Action Step Two hadn't just failed, it had gone up in spectacular, special-effect flames. Up the beach, I could see Mom hand Eileen a sign-up sheet. Eileen stretched out her hand, shook her head, and handed it back. That would be a no. Zero for zero for the Gillis Girls.

I felt a tug on my arm. Josh stood next to me, looking up with a frown.

"It's Charlotte Boulay," he said. "Maddy's talking about Charlotte Boulay."

"What about her?" I asked, but Josh didn't answer. Carefully, he took off his SpongeBob floaties and handed them to me.

"You should take these," he said. "So you feel safe."

11

SPLASH!

For the next three days, I set my alarm for five thirty to figure out the source of the splash. After the depressing events at swim lessons, I needed it to be something good. One of those incredible, amazing things Mom had promised would happen at The Showboat Resort. It could be an otter doing a backflip. Or a moose with huge antlers going for a swim. Even if it was something terrible—a wolf with fangs drowning its kill—I had to know.

The first morning, I climbed onto the window seat and fell asleep until eight.

The second morning, I was distracted by a nest I spotted high up in the tree next to the loft. I didn't know it was a nest at first. It looked like a mess of twigs and leaves that had gotten caught in the branches of the tree. A squirrel scurried across the branch, and I wondered if it was something he'd built. I would have thought squirrels lived in tunnels, or tree hollows, or . . . *SPLASH!* I turned my head too late. The water rippled and left no trace.

The third morning, I was focused. I watched the dock even when the squirrel started chattering and throwing things from his nest to the ground. When I felt my eyes closing, I pinched myself and patted my cheeks to wake up. And finally, I saw it. The shock of orange hair. Arms lifting to the sky. The dive. The splash. The widening circles of water.

At first, I felt numb. After all that. Being woken up, terrified, every dawn for the last six days. The splash was Charlotte Boulay going for a swim.

It wasn't terrifying.

It certainly wasn't magical.

Except: I waited five minutes, then ten. A bird with spindly legs and a long neck flew down from a tree and landed on the dock, but the orange-haired woman never emerged from the lake.

12

HONK FOR ASSISTANCE

I talked myself out of it ten different times, but after lunch, I shrugged my backpack onto my shoulders and told Mom I was going outside to explore.

"See? You're going to love it here!" Mom looked relieved. I'd spent most of the week holed up in the cabin, re-reading old comics and helping Mom sort through her database for untapped Potentials. Neither of us was having much fun. "Need extra bug spray?"

I shook my head. What I needed was another look at Charlotte Boulay—for three reasons. I wanted to know if she was still alive, for one. Or had Thunder Lake swallowed her up? For two, I wanted to know what Josh was talking about. Why were they all so skittish about Charlotte? She was odd, but she didn't seem scary. In comics, humans are always freaking out about mutants who are perfectly interesting and nice—and have cool powers to boot. That could be Charlotte. The risk, of course, is that sometimes mutants are terrifying monsters who want to destroy the world. It's not always easy to tell which is which.

The third reason I wanted another look at Charlotte Boulay was that I was completely, utterly, and powerfully bored out of my skull.

I tucked a Honey Bee Wrinkle-Free sample pack in the main pocket of my backpack, and even though I didn't believe any of Maddy's watch-your-back hype, I put Josh's floaties in, too. I stepped out into the pine air and headed down the path to the hotel.

The front office was dead quiet. I blinked and tried to adjust my eyes to the pink glow of the mermaid lamp.

"Hello?" My voice hung in the air.

I unzipped my backpack and forced happy thoughts into my brain. *It's cozy in here, not creepy. Charlotte Boulay will love these samples. They'll probably get rid of all her wrinkles and she'll buy so many bottles that Mom will skip Queen Bee and get promoted all the way to Vice President.*

I set the sample pack on the front desk and noticed a tiny sign propped up on a miniature easel.

HONK FOR ASSISTANCE

Next to the sign was an antique silver horn with a black rubber bulb at the end. I squeezed the bulb, but the horn didn't honk. It gave a soft *whoosh* of air, then something clattered loudly behind me. My stomach leaped to my throat. Slowly, I turned to face the mermaid lamp. It stood perfectly still in front of the bookshelf, the life-size tail shimmering, ivory arms holding the pink lampshade like a halo. The mermaid stared straight ahead at a picture frame that had fallen off the wall.

I turned to pick it up. It wasn't broken. The frame and glass were made out of some sort of heavy-duty plastic. Inside, an old black-and-white photograph showed two boys in white tuxedoes tap-dancing on top of a grand piano. Written across the photo were the words: *To Mr. & Mrs. B—Thanks for keeping the dream alive! —Buck & Bubbles.*

When I turned back to face the front desk, a new sign was propped up on the tiny easel:

I SAID, **HONK** FOR ASSISTANCE

"Hello?" I called out again. "Ms. Boulay?"

I weighed my options. There weren't many: A) honk, or B) leave. My hand shook a little as I squeezed the bulb, and the horn wheezed. I squeezed it harder. It wheezed with a half-hearted squeak at the end.

Another frame crashed to the ground, and my stomach

lurched again. It was another old photo, but this one gave me a shiver. The woman in the picture looked normal enough—wide smile, long eyelashes, glamorous dress. Her arms were stretched out like she was about to give someone a big, lovey hug. Except all down those outstretched arms perched a line of small white mice. There had to be twenty mice balancing on each arm, and the woman was smiling like she was about to take them for a walk in the park. The signature read: *For The Showboat—a true diamond in the rough! XOXO, Lady Alice and her Dirty Rats.*

Before hanging the photo back up, I checked out the hook it had been hanging on. When pressed, there was some sort of quick-release mechanism that made it pull back into the wall. Someone—or some*thing*—must have been releasing the frames when I squeezed the horn.

There was a scraping noise on the desk behind me. Without thinking, I held Lady Alice's picture above my head like a weapon and turned around fast.

I was too late. A third sign was propped up on the desk easel.

FOR HEAVEN'S SAKE, I CAN'T HEAR YOU

I hung Lady Alice back on the wall and, as quietly as I could, tiptoed toward the desk. This had to be another one of Charlotte Boulay's weird jokes. I was sure she was crouched behind the desk, cracking herself up over her tricks. I tried to stay calm as I kneeled at the corner and waited a few seconds, listening. When I couldn't wait any longer, I lunged behind the desk.

"Gotcha!" I shouted.

To nobody.

I searched around for a door or passageway that might lead to a different room, but the only door out was the one I came in. There was nothing behind the desk except for the wall of books, the old woman's step stool, and a broom.

I stood on the stool. The room seemed different from this angle. All the photos, floor to ceiling, stared straight at me—hundreds of eyes watching me like a black-and-white audience of ghosts from the past. I felt weirdly embarrassed, and let my eyes drop to the desk. Charlotte's calendar lay there, open to the month of June. I stepped down from the stool to get a better look.

The calendar was practically blank. *Carrie & Anthoni Gillis* were the only guests listed all month long. I turned the page to July. Nothing. August, September. I closed the book—no one was staying here but us.

It wasn't a mind-blowing surprise, but still. The empty pages made me think about all the hours I'd spent dreaming about The Showboat Resort. All the things Mom and I did to try to get here. The miles, the makeovers, the

Next Hive Destinations. It was all supposed to be worth it. Now it seemed like a hoax.

My eyes stung, and I tried to shake it off. It wasn't a big deal if there weren't other *kids* at The Showboat. I'd already found my Best Potential, and even if our first encounter hadn't gone so well, first impressions weren't everything. When Rogue wanted to join the X-Men, everyone hated her, especially Storm. But Rogue worked hard to earn their trust and prove she was a true friend. I didn't need more Potentials. I just needed the chance to prove myself.

But Mom? We only had six weeks to get back on track and if *nobody* was coming to the resort . . . I sighed. Positive Thoughts Attract Positive Results. I tried to change my state. Mom could find Potentials anywhere. The beach. The Little Store. The church. I didn't have to worry. Mom would pay back Mr. Li. She'd figure it out. She'd cheer up and find a place for us to live. It might be great, really—another fresh start. This time, we'd do it right, and we wouldn't have to stress about groceries or rent. The best part was that I'd have Maddy. We'd visit and spend summers together, and it wouldn't matter if no one sat by me at lunch because I'd have a True Blue Friend for life, and she'd always show up when needed.

It was fine. It was all going to be fine.

A drop of water fell onto the cover of the calendar, and

I rubbed it out with my finger, swallowing and blinking until the threat of more tears went away. When I lifted my head, I saw Charlotte Boulay's orange hair aglow under the mermaid lamp.

She cleared her throat.

"Looking for *me*, my dear?"

13

HUMBUG

Charlotte's hand was on the elbow of the mermaid lamp. It looked like they were old pals having a chat. I came out from behind the desk.

"You're supposed to honk for assistance." She pointed to the sign.

Her flyaway hair was slicked back in a tight orange bun, and she was wearing a man's tuxedo with a sparkly butterfly brooch pinned to the lapel. She acted like nothing strange had been happening at all.

"I tried," I said, hoping my voice didn't sound as shaky as it felt. "It doesn't work."

"Oh, it works," she said with a knowing nod. "That's not at all what's wrong with it."

"It's not?"

She shook her head sadly. "The poor thing."

She brushed past me, stepped behind the desk, and stroked the horn as if it were a lonely cat. Her eyes flicked to the calendar I'd been examining, then, with a shake of her head, she brought her attention back to the horn.

"After all these years . . . this old horn just doesn't give a hoot."

She slapped her hands in a *ba-dum-bum!* rhythm on the desk. "Ha!" she cried.

My mouth hung open.

"Doesn't give a hoot! Get it? The horn?" She gave the horn a wheezy squeeze.

I was so stunned that I didn't even feel the laugh coming. It burst out of my throat, shattering the gloom that had been gathering around me. My eyes stopped burning, and Charlotte Boulay nodded triumphantly, like she knew the laugh was there all along.

"You're not a bad audience, kid," she said. "Now, what's the story, morning glory? What can I do ya for?"

I pointed to the Honey Bee Wrinkle-Free sample pack I'd set on the desk.

"It's for you," I said. "In case you want to give it a try."

She plucked a monocle out of the breast pocket of her tuxedo and held it up to her eye. As she examined the samples, her giant, watery eyeball roamed back and forth behind the lens.

"It's got three things," I said. "Night Cream, Day Cream, and None of Your Beeswax! Age Eraser." I tried to make my voice sound chirpy and cheerful like Mom's. "There's a sale going on right now, but if you like the products, the best thing to do is to sign up to be a Worker Bee. That way, you get the deepest discount, plus you have the opportunity to sell the products to your own friends and clients. It's a win-win."

Mom's sales pitch flowed out of my mouth. I was killing time. I didn't even know what I wanted to ask, let alone how to ask it. *Hey, Charlotte, why do the kids at the beach act like you're a man-eating alien? You know how you jumped in the water this morning? How come I didn't see you get out? Or come up for air, even? Want to explain that to me?*

Charlotte focused the monocle on me and blinked her mutant eye.

"Hm," she said. "It's a decent pitch, but not great."

The monocle magnified her wrinkles, turning them into small mountain ranges.

"Look, kid, your audience is never wrong. If you can't hook 'em, you've either got a problem with your material or your delivery isn't good. Now, try again—you really think this 'Age Eraser' will work?"

She dropped the monocle back in her pocket and leaned across the desk, resting her chin on her hands, waiting.

"Um . . . I . . ."

"Chop-chop!" Charlotte barked. "What is this, a staring contest?"

"I don't think it will work," I blurted. "You have too many wrinkles."

Charlotte threw her hands up in the air and groaned. "Awful!" she cried. "Terrible! Kids these days!" She paced in a circle behind the desk, then swung around to face me. "This," she said, picking up the sample pack, "is the single most important product you will ever buy in your life! Not only will it smooth tired wrinkles, it will transport you—see, 'transport' is always a good word; people want to be transported—it will transport you to the vigor, vitality, and vim of your youth! If you don't feel ten years younger after one week of using this marvelous cream, you can have your money back—one hundred percent guaranteed!"

She set down the cream. "Eh?" she said. "Better?"

"So if it doesn't work, you'd have to give everyone's money back?"

Charlotte Boulay shook her finger at me. "Ah, but you won't have to. You're selling them what they want to believe." Her eyes drifted to the wall behind my head. "It's showbiz," she said. "But it ain't what it used to be."

I followed her gaze to the wall of photos. "Do you know all these people?" I asked.

"Some," she said. "My parents knew them all. They were hoofers. Song-and-dance folks."

"Did you dance, too?" I asked.

Charlotte narrowed her eyes and her voice took on a hard, sarcastic tone. "If it made money for The *Great* Frank and Selina Boulay." She said the word "great" like it was an insult. "Those two always had a scheme. New city. New plan. New humbug. People ate it up."

"Didn't you like it?"

Charlotte stiffened.

"Of course I did!" she snapped. "It was electrifying!" An odd growling sound came from her throat. "But believe me, it gets old."

Charlotte started fidgeting with the broom behind the desk, twirling the handle with her fingers. Her mood had changed into something dark and sad, and I got the distinct feeling I should drop the subject, but all of a sudden I wanted to know everything. What it was like to be a "hoofer," hanging out with tap dancers and white mice. Whether her grandfather was really a ventriloquist *and* a trick bicyclist. Charlotte's world was so bizarre and fascinating, I almost felt . . . transported.

"What's a humbug?" I asked.

Spit gathered at the sides of her mouth, and she twirled the broom handle faster. "A hoax. A trick to get people to part with their money. Don't look at me like that. It's not so different from your Age Eraser, if you want to know!"

The broom clattered to the floor, and Charlotte's stare shot through me like a laser blast from Cyclops. She pushed the Honey Bee Wrinkle-Free sample pack across the desk toward me.

"Like I said, you sell them what they want to believe." She paused. "I don't feel like talking anymore. I'm an old lady and I'm tired. I think it's time for you to go."

I put the wrinkle cream in my backpack, but I didn't leave. Charlotte Boulay was the weirdest, most interesting person I'd ever met, and I wanted to see what she did next. Besides, I was certain she had snuck into the room through some kind of door, window, or secret compartment. I wasn't going to take my eye off her until I saw her go out the same way.

Charlotte took a handkerchief out of her pocket, turned her back to me, and started furiously cleaning the glass on a picture of a man eating a cigarette. Her orange bun jiggled on the back of her head.

I didn't move.

She turned her head halfway around to look at me, then quickly snapped her attention back to the wall.

I waited.

She held the handkerchief in midair.

"Well?" she said to the wall. "Why aren't you leaving?"

"Why aren't *you* leaving?" I asked.

She put the handkerchief in her pocket and turned to face me.

"Because I live here." A curly strand of hair had slipped out of her slick bun, and it bounced on top of her head like an orange question mark.

I bit the inside of my cheek and held my ground. "I want to see how you came in," I said.

Charlotte stepped out from behind the desk and positioned herself next to the mermaid lamp. It cast a spooky light across her face, giving her nose and chin sharp angles that hadn't been there before.

"Little girl," she said slowly, her eyes piercing mine. "I would like you to leave now."

My knees went wobbly, but I stayed.

"Suit yourself," she said, quiet as a whisper. Charlotte Boulay reached out a bony hand and closed it around the mermaid lamp.

Click.

The room went dark.

14

THE BLACK BEAR

By the time I felt my way to the door, pulled it open, and let the sunshine flood in, the front office was empty. The mermaid lamp smiled innocently, but there was not one trace of Charlotte Boulay.

I forced myself to take slow, normal steps back down the path until I hit the woods. Then I sprinted toward the Showboat cabins, my backpack slapping against my shoulders, blood pounding in my head. What had just happened? I liked that Charlotte was dramatic and unpredictable, but when she flicked off the light, I felt like I'd run into Mr. Sinister in a dark alley without Storm or Wolverine anywhere near to help.

I stopped to catch my breath at The Black Bear. A wooden statue of a bear cub stood on his hind legs near the porch of the cabin. His paws were outstretched like he was waiting for someone to set a big tray of honey in his arms.

My hands were shaking, so I stuffed them in my sweat-shirt pocket and sat down on the ground, leaning my head against the wooden cub. I felt a little silly, getting spooked by a dark room, but my heart was beating like a rabbit's. *Breathe, Anthoni, breathe. Think happy thoughts*. I couldn't think of any. I had to go with the basics. *Ice cream. Mint chocolate-chip ice cream. Mint chocolate-chip ice cream in a waffle cone*. A chipmunk scurried out from behind a tree and grabbed a pinecone a few feet away from me. I watched him shove piece after piece of it into his mouth, his cheeks stretching like lumpy balloons.

A loud *snap* sent the chipmunk skittering away, and I jumped to my feet. Something shuffled on the far side of the porch.

I picked up the heaviest stick I could find and backed up slowly, until I had a view around the corner of the cabin. There was definitely something there.

"Meow," it said. But it wasn't a cat. It was a person, crouched low to the ground, with a tree branch in front of his face.

"Hey!" I yelled, braver than I felt.

DJ let out a yelp and jumped into the air. He held his cast in front of his face for protection, then slowly let it down. The freckles on his face had become one giant tomato-red blotch, and he gave me a look somewhere between a grimace and a grin.

"That was freaky," he said, clearly embarrassed.

"You scared the wits out of me!" I yelled. "What are you doing? *Following* me?"

The boy shrugged. "A little." His freckles got even redder.

My mouth hung open. What kind of person sneaks around spying on people in the middle of the woods?

"I saw you go up there," he said, pointing at The Showboat. "Did you see her? Is she as scary as they say?"

"You live here. Haven't *you* seen her?"

He shook his head. "Not once, and I've been living in my aunt's house for a whole year—right over there." He pointed into the woods, away from The Black Bear and The Showboat, but the trees were too thick to see any sort of house.

We stood there awkwardly. DJ dug a line in the dirt with his toe.

"Sorry I scared you," he said. "The kids around here make it out like she's half vampire or something." He paused and studied his dirt line. "They're probably just messing with me 'cause I'm not from here."

"She's not a vampire," I said, "but she *is* strange."

He brightened a little. "Good strange or bad strange?"

Great question. "I'm not sure yet."

"Wanna see something weird?" DJ asked.

"Okay."

"You'll have to hold your nose."

DJ stepped onto the porch of The Black Bear and jiggled the screen door until it creaked open.

"Are you allowed to go in there?" I asked.

"Kind of, well, not really . . . but no one's using it." DJ felt along the side of the door until he found a key.

"How'd you know that was there?"

He raised a shoulder in an uncomfortable shrug. I know there are people who can't help blushing, but this kid's face went from white to red and back again faster than a blinking stoplight. He didn't answer. Instead, he pulled the neck of his shirt up over his nose, held up his cast, and said, "Ready?"

As soon as the door swung open, a sour, musty smell wafted out of the house. It hit me so hard it brought tears to my eyes. I threw my hand over my nose.

"What *is* it?" I yelled through my hand.

DJ ran straight for the back bedroom. I knew I should leave. Not only were we breaking and entering, but anything that smelled that bad couldn't be worth it. Still, I held my nose and followed him into the cabin.

DJ shut the bedroom door behind us.

"You have to get through the front fast," he gasped. "It doesn't smell as bad back here."

I took my hand off my face. He was right.

"What is it?" I asked. "A dead animal?"

DJ shot me a serious stare. "I don't want to find out," he said.

The Black Bear was the mirror image of The Blue Heron. The room we were standing in was identical to Mom's room. The same wicker furniture, the same moose wallpaper—but the window was on the opposite side of the bed. DJ tried to push at it one-handed. I helped him open it, and he sucked in the fresh air dramatically.

I looked around the room. "I take it you wanted to show me some rocks?"

The bed and the dresser were covered with small piles of rocks. Some were organized by size, but others seemed to be grouped together by color or shape. There had to be hundreds of them in the room.

"No, that's my collection," DJ said. "My aunt said I had to get it out of the house, but I didn't want to leave it outside. That's why I figured out how to get in here."

"I don't blame her. It's a lot of rocks." I picked up a handful of black-and-white speckled specimens.

"Those are intrusive igneous granite," DJ said. "They crystalized from magma millions of years ago. But check this out."

He walked to the closet and opened the door. In the corner hung three massive fur coats. One of them looked like it had come straight off a bear.

"I think those were swanky back in the day," DJ said. He reached under the coats and pulled out a round, dusty hatbox with a butterfly on top.

"Ta-da!"

He lifted the lid with a flourish. Beady black eyes and sharp yellow teeth grimaced up at me. I yelped.

"I think it's a scarf," DJ said with a grin. "Isn't it disgusting? I screamed like a three-year-old when I saw it. But don't worry. It's not alive."

He draped the long animal pelt around his neck, and held the head out for me to see. The thing was basically a long, furry strip of skin that had been sliced right off the back of an animal. With the head still attached. I touched the hard, black nose and ran my fingers down the pelt. It was silky soft and absolutely revolting.

The butterfly box was lined with newspaper. I grabbed a handful to wipe off any rabies germs I might have contracted.

"There's more stuff in here," I said.

DJ leaned closer as I pulled out some yellow ribbons, a crocheted butterfly, and a collection of tiny glass animal figurines. I set them on the floor and reached for the last item in the hatbox: a black-and-white photo in a silver frame.

DJ dropped the dead animal head.

The photo was shot at a beach. A tall man, a woman, and a tiny little girl smiled huge, movie-star smiles. The woman and the girl wore identical bikini tops and their hairdos matched perfectly except for the star-shaped barrette holding back the girl's bangs. The woman and the man stood on each side of the girl, lifting her by the arms so she dangled in the air between them. If you only saw the top half of the frame, it would be an everyday, cute family photo. The bottom half was a different story.

Instead of legs, the little girl had a shiny, scaly mermaid tail. Not like a costume you would wear for Halloween. Like a fish.

There was writing on the top of the photo. In small, loopy cursive, it read: *May 17, 1933. Introducing the world to our greatest discovery—Baby Charlotte, the Boulay Mermaid.*

DJ whistled through his teeth. "Is that her?" he asked.

I studied the photo, trying to recognize Charlotte Boulay's angled nose and chin on the little mermaid's chubby face. Charlotte had told me her parents liked hoaxes, but the picture didn't look fake.

"It's almost like they photoshopped it," DJ said. He picked up the animal head again and shook it back and forth. He made the beady eyes look straight into mine.

"But they didn't have Photoshop in 1933," the animal pelt said in DJ's squeaky voice. The head came closer and the dead whiskers brushed my chin.

"That's disgusting," I said.

I put the ribbons and figurines back into the box with

the newspapers, but I didn't let go of the Boulay Mermaid. I needed to look at it longer. When I was by myself and had time to think.

"I'm going to borrow this," I said, unzipping my backpack. I tucked the frame underneath Josh's floaties.

DJ smirked at me. "Are you *allowed* to do that?"

"Are you *allowed* to keep your rock collection in here?" It might not be a great idea, but I felt desperate to study the photo. And who was I going to ask? Charlotte?

"I'll bring it back," I said. "Tomorrow. Does anyone else come in here?"

"Squirrels."

I stood up, opened the bedroom door, and got hit head-on by the horrible smell. I slammed the door shut again and set my backpack on the bed.

"DJ, if I'm coming back here, we have to find out what that smell is."

DJ squeezed his eyes tight, and made a pained, groaning noise in the back of his throat. Finally, he opened his eyes and shoved the nasty animal pelt back into the hatbox.

"Fine," he said. "But if it's something actually dead and not skinned, I'll probably run. Just so you know."

We covered our faces and I opened the door. The smell was coming from the kitchen. The cupboards were coated in dust and grime, but there wasn't anything inside.

"Okay," I said from behind my hand. "It's got to be the fridge."

When DJ opened the refrigerator, the smell hit us harder than one of Magneto's force fields. The shelves were empty, but there was a milk container in the door. DJ pulled it out with his good hand, fumbled it, and dropped it. A thick, brown-green liquid oozed out onto the linoleum.

DJ took one look at it and puked on the floor. I felt my gut convulse, and I turned around and ran. I managed to get out the door and down the porch stairs before vomiting all over the feet of the sad wooden bear cub.

DJ flew out the door behind me and threw himself on the ground, rolling in the pine needles. He groaned, hollered, and flailed around like he was trying to shake the smell off. Finally, he writhed one last time, threw all of his limbs in the air, then flopped them down to the ground. He lay flat with his arms and legs splayed out, and stared up at the trees.

"I found the smell," he said.

15

CLEANING HOUSE

Whatcha doin', Anthoni?" Mom asked without looking up from her laptop screen.

"I need plastic bags. And some cleaning supplies."

"Under the sink." Her fingers stopped typing long enough for her to add, "Good news: we still don't have cell service, but I got us internet today. Now I can keep in touch with all my Worker Bees."

That was a relief. She needed to do everything she could to inspire her team toward a month-end sales boost. I had a brief urge to tell her about the mermaid photo and how DJ and I had broken into The Black Bear and puked all over it. A few days ago, I would have. But now that Mom had broken the Gillis Girls Tell Each Other Everything rule, I felt like breaking it, too.

"Good luck, Mom," I said, and closed the screen door behind me.

When I got back to The Black Bear, all the windows were wide open and DJ had taken off his shirt and tied it around his face. His arms were sunburned, but his belly was blindingly white and he waggled his eyebrows at me above his T-shirt mask. He looked ridiculous. I dumped the cleaning supplies on the porch and DJ stretched a blue plastic glove over his cast, completing the fashion statement.

"I'll clean the fridge, but I'm not touching your puke," I said.

We used half a bottle of Mom's Organic Grapefruit Cleanser removing ten-year-old milk from the floor and the refrigerator. DJ had to go outside and upchuck two more times, but he shook it off and got right back to work.

It might be abnormal, but I like cleaning. Every time Mom and I moved to a new apartment, we gave it a top-to-bottom deep clean. Each room we finished felt fresh and new, filled with possibility and promise.

Once DJ and I had cleaned the fridge and the floor, the rest of the kitchen seemed that much grimier and more depressing. I didn't want to leave it like that. I didn't want to leave, period. To do what? Sit in The Blue Heron while Mom sent emails to her team? I climbed onto the counter and started scrubbing the cabinets.

"What are you doing?" DJ asked. "I didn't puke on those."

"We should have done these first," I said. "If you want to clean a room efficiently, you have to start from the top down. Otherwise, you knock dirt and dust onto areas you've already cleaned, and clearly that's a waste of time."

"Clearly?" DJ asked, wide-eyed. But he found a feather duster and a broom in the closet and galloped around the cabin while I scrubbed, pretending he was a one-handed sorcerer destroying villages of dust mites with his powerful wand. In one of the more heated battles, he used a hanging chair as a catapult and almost pulled down the curtains.

"You're really strange, DJ," I said, wiping down the last of the cupboards.

"Good strange or bad strange?" he asked. He still had his T-shirt wrapped around his face and the blue glove covering his cast.

I shook my head. "I have no idea."

By the time we were done, we had a garbage bag full of stinky paper towels and one impressively clean cabin. We tied up the bag, dragged it outside, and tossed it in the metal garbage bin by the woodpile. Then we stood staring at the wooden bear. Even with vomit at his feet, I thought the cub looked a little cheerier. I smiled at him and gave his paw a high-five.

"Well, Gills." DJ's freckles disappeared into his tomato-soup blush, and he gave me an awkward salute. "It's been weird to know you. See you later, maybe."

He ran into the woods, tripped on a stick, and took a face-plant.

"I'm good!" he called. He waved his T-shirt in the air and galloped away.

Mom was still typing at the picnic table in the kitchen when I walked in the door of The Blue Heron.

"Guess who I ran into at the Little Store today?" she asked.

"Elmo?"

"Someone's feeling happier," Mom said with a smile. "I told you exploring would be fun."

"It was okay," I said. But she was right. I did feel better.

"I saw Mary Quinn and Julie's mom, Anna Lee. Mary invited us all to their log cabin for dinner tonight. She said we're supposed to bring our swimsuits."

"Great." I turned away from her and put what was left of the Grapefruit Cleanser under the sink so she wouldn't see the disappointment on my face. I knew I should be excited to move to the next Action Step in my plan, but I hadn't figured out how I was going to win over Maddy Quinn. And I was really hoping I wouldn't have to do it in a swimsuit.

"It's a good opportunity for both of us to develop some Potentials, you know."

"I know," I said. "It's just . . . Maddy isn't as nice as I expected."

"She doesn't know you yet. Find out what she likes. Make a connection. She'll come around."

"She likes X-Men."

"Really? Then you're set."

"I know. But . . ." I didn't want to attract negative results, so I didn't say the rest out loud: What if she doesn't like *me*?

Mom knew what I was thinking anyway. She came over and ran her fingers through my bangs, fluffing them to the side. "Of course she'll like you. Who *wouldn't* like you? And Julie will be there. She seems nice. Besides," Mom chucked my chin with her fist. "You're a tough cookie. You can make this work."

She had a point. If I could survive being left in the dark by Charlotte Boulay, stalked in the woods by a camouflage-obsessed boy, and lured into a cabin filled with vomit and moldy milk, I could handle a few small Action Steps. All I had to do was remind Maddy how fun I was, point out how much we had in common, and prove to her that I could earn her trust. Once I did, it would be smooth sailing.

Mom wrinkled her nose and sniffed in my direction. "You should take a shower, though. You smell funny."

She sniffed again. "You didn't go in the lake, did you? No swimming without an adult, right? That's our deal." Her nose twitched, and she kept sniffing around me like a dog looking for bones.

"Mom!" I wiggled away from her. "Stop smelling me. I'm not getting in that lake unless I have to. I promise."

It wasn't until after I'd scrubbed myself clean and was sitting in the Beemobile on my way to Maddy Quinn's that I remembered the photo of the Boulay Mermaid. My backpack! I couldn't remember carrying it home.

"I need to run back for a minute," I said. I tried to think through exactly where DJ had found the key to The Black Bear and how he'd jiggled the screen door open. If I was lucky, he'd accidentally left it unlocked.

Mom laughed like I'd told a funny joke.

"For real," I said. "I'll be fast. It's my *backpack*." I knew we'd already driven halfway around Thunder Lake, but Mom would understand. She knew I kept all my important stuff in my backpack. She'd once driven three hours in the wrong direction when I forgot it at a truck stop in Michigan. She wouldn't mind going back one measly mile. I did a quick inventory of what was in it now. My notebook. Josh's floaties. The Boulay Mermaid.

"You'll have to do without it tonight," Mom said. "We're here."

She turned the car down a tiny road marked *Private— No Hunting* and entered a circular driveway. A low whistle escaped from her lips.

"Some cabin!"

Maddy Quinn's house was built out of logs, but other than that, it looked nothing like a log cabin. It was three stories high with huge bay windows and a stone chimney that took up one whole side of the house.

Mrs. Quinn answered the door holding her phone to her ear, and waved us in. "How awful," she said into the phone. "You poor thing!"

She nodded for us to follow her into a living room with high wooden beams in the ceiling. An entire wall of windows faced Thunder Lake. It felt like a cathedral. Mom and I gazed at the view, the stone fireplace, and the grand piano as Mrs. Quinn finished up her call. I wondered which B&B samples Mom had brought. The Quinns could clearly afford the Premium package.

"That was Anna Lee," Mrs. Quinn said. "Julie and her brother got into some poison ivy, and they're not going to be able to make it tonight."

I'd been aware there could be bears or rogue woodsmen in the forest, but it hadn't even *occurred* to me that I needed to watch out for poison ivy. The backs of my knees felt itchy just thinking about it.

Mrs. Quinn crossed her arms, then uncrossed them. I wasn't sure if she wanted us to stay or go now that the Lees weren't coming. She shook her long, glamorous ponytail at me. "Maddy will still be glad you're here."

I smiled politely and hoped she was right.

16

TRICK SKIS

Mrs. Quinn led us up a staircase into the greatest bedroom I'd ever seen. The bed was shaped like a giant marshmallow, and the wall behind it was painted with an X-Men mural. On one side of the bed stood Storm, larger than life with her hands on her hips, white hair and cape billowing behind her. On the other side of the bed was Emma Frost in her diamond form. Mom caught my eye and gave me a thumbs-up. The Quinns had some serious Potential.

"Maddy," Mrs. Quinn called. "Carrie and Anthoni are here. Let's go take them for a ski."

Maddy peeked out from behind a door that I'd thought was a closet. She was wearing rectangular glasses that she hadn't worn at the beach.

"I don't think Anthoni skis, Mom."

"She's right," I said, and bristled in case a mean laugh or a comment about my bubble-blowing abilities was coming my way.

Instead, she said, "Hi, Anthoni." Like we were old pals.

Mrs. Quinn turned to Mom. "Carrie, you're probably dying to get behind the boat."

"I haven't . . . I'm out of practice . . ." Mom stumbled for an excuse and landed on: "I forgot my suit."

Mrs. Quinn waved her hand. "I have dozens. Maddy, you and Anthoni go find your dad in the boathouse. We'll meet you at the dock after we've changed."

The boathouse turned out to be exactly what it sounded like: an entire house for a boat. A shiny speedboat with the words *Ski Nautique* on the side hung suspended from the ceiling by two thick cables. A tan, muscled man with a bald head and sunglasses stood on a wooden platform pushing a lever that slowly lowered the boat toward the water. When he saw us, he let go of the lever and the boat swayed in midair.

"Nice to see you, sport." Maddy's dad led us into a small room in the back of the boathouse where skis and life jackets lined the walls. He passed two short, fat skis to Maddy.

"Do the trick-ski routine," he said. "Your transitions could use some work."

He turned to me. "What's your style, Anthoni? Trick? Slalom? Or are you a daredevil like your mom?"

I felt like I was in swim class all over again, listening to a language I didn't understand. He must have Mom confused with someone else. She was a lot of things, but "daredevil" wasn't one of them.

"Anthoni doesn't ski, Dad," Maddy said. Again, I waited for a snide comment, but it didn't come.

Mr. Quinn looked surprised, but he winked and tossed me a red life jacket. When I got my arms through, he zipped it up and tightened the straps until I felt like my ribs might cave in.

"I'm good," I wheezed.

"Then let's get this show on the road!"

We stood on the wooden platform while Mr. Quinn lowered the boat until the bottom half bobbed in the water. He hopped down into the *Ski Nautique* and Maddy jumped in behind him with a *thud*. Mr. Quinn held his hand out to me. I didn't budge. I watched the boat bounce and sway in the murky water and I thought I might be sick for the second time that day.

Maddy held her hand out, too. "We've got you."

She sounded like she meant it. I gave myself a pep talk. I wasn't getting in the water. I only had to sit in the boat and watch other people ski. How bad could it be? I took their outstretched hands and let them lift me down.

I flinched as the boat sputtered to a start, and Mr. Quinn winked at me again.

"Nothing to fear," he said. "I drove the boat when your mom was a Waterbug on the ski team. I'm a pro."

He backed gently out of the boathouse and putted along the shore. I let myself relax. Maddy and I sat on a comfy vinyl seat, sturdy and safe. It wasn't bad at all. Then her dad hit the throttle.

The nose of the boat flew into the air, and a startled scream escaped from my throat. We hurtled toward the middle of the lake at an insane speed. The wind whipped my hair into my face, and Maddy's log cabin grew smaller behind us. Without warning, Mr. Quinn turned the boat in a tight circle, a full 360 degrees.

I slid down the seat and crashed into Maddy. To my surprise, she grabbed my arm and screamed bloody murder right along with me as water sprayed around us. Once we'd gone full circle, the boat hit the waves we'd made and we bounced over them, the *Ski Nautique* flying higher and higher into the air with each wave. Maddy and I clutched each other and screamed louder, sliding from the bench seat to the carpeted floor of the boat. My knee knocked into her elbow, and the vibration of the boat's motor made my screams wobble and shake like a jackhammer.

I wished I could freeze the moment in time, holding everything in place—the speedboat, Maddy's mouth opened in a comic-book scream, the white froth on the waves, the sparkle of the sun glinting off the spray—I wanted to capture it, and hold it, and never let it end. Because right there, flying over Thunder Lake, something magical happened. Maddy Quinn and I locked eyes, and exactly like two six-year-olds screaming at Gramps's dragon impression, we started to laugh. We screamed and laughed until tears ran down my cheeks, and I swear I'd never felt lighter or happier in my life.

Abruptly, Mr. Quinn slowed the boat to turtle speed and putted back toward the dock.

"Still works," Mr. Quinn said with a sly grin.

When we reached the dock, Maddy and I untangled ourselves, and she hopped into the water with her skis. Her dad tossed her a long multicolored rope while Mom and Mrs. Quinn stepped into the boat and sandwiched me on the bench seat.

"Up to your old tricks, I see, Leon," Mom said.

Maddy held on to the ski rope and floated in the water, getting her skis into position. When she yelled, "Hit it!" Mr. Quinn accelerated and Maddy stood up on the skis like it was as easy as getting out of bed. She held the rope with one hand while she adjusted her swimsuit with the other, then she did two 180-degree turns in a row. When she lifted her foot in the air, one of her skis fell off. No one else seemed to notice.

"She lost a ski!" I shouted over the engine.

Mr. Quinn gave me a thumbs-up.

After that, it got crazy. Maddy held one foot and one arm in the air like a ballet dancer, and wobbled until she caught her balance. Then she hooked the handle of the rope onto her foot. Her ski swerved from side to side like she might fall, but she steadied herself and skied on one foot with no hands while we passed the public beach. When we got close to the bay and The Showboat Resort, Mr. Quinn made a wide, slow turn and headed back home. Maddy released her foot and tumbled into the water right in front of the dock. Her second ski had washed up onto the shore.

"I'll go next!" Mrs. Quinn dove into the lake, and Maddy climbed into the boat, shivering.

Mr. Quinn threw a towel around her. "What happened to the tricks in the second half? You don't get to be the best by riding it out, Mads."

Maddy winced like the words hurt her, and I wanted to yell at her dad. His daughter had water-skied around an entire lake *on one foot*. She was amazing.

Mom helped Mr. Quinn change the ski rope and Maddy sat down on the seat next to me, dripping water everywhere. There was a red mark on her foot where the rope handle had been—no wonder this girl thought I was a chicken for not wanting to put my head in the lake.

"You're really good," I said.

"Thanks. I have to practice a lot." The sun came out from behind a cloud and she squinted at me. "How do you and Julie know each other so well?"

I shook my head. "We don't."

"We're best friends," she said. "Just so you know."

I breathed a sigh of relief. That was it. Julie was the reason Maddy had been so mean at the beach. She thought I was going to steal *Julie* from her. Which I definitely was not. It was all a misunderstanding, and now we could start over. We already had.

The sun beamed harder, warming my back, and Maddy shaded her eyes with her hand.

"We've been best friends for two years."

"That's great," I said, and I meant it. It *was* great. I didn't mind if Maddy and Julie were best friends. It wasn't the same thing at all. Best friends come and go. True Blue is forever.

"Don't worry," I started. "I'm not . . ."

Before I could finish, Mom sat down next to us and Mrs. Quinn shouted, "Hit it!" The boat took off, drowning out my voice in the roar of the engine.

Mrs. Quinn skied on one long ski and zoomed from one side of the boat's wake to the other. She leaned into each turn, sending a tall spray of water into the air, bending her knees as her ski skimmed over each wake. The sun caught the spray and made knee-high rainbows in the sky. Zoom to the right. Spray. Zoom to the left.

Spray. The muscles in her arms bulged like Emma Frost's. I could have watched her all day.

When it was Mom's turn, she handed me her sunglasses and her shirt, but crossed her arms nervously over her suit.

"I haven't skied since college," she said.

Mr. Quinn handed her a life jacket. "It's like riding a bike, Gills. You never forget."

Gills? I shot Maddy a look. She seemed deeply interested in her toenails.

Mom laughed as if she *liked* the nickname.

"I always tell Maddy she should be like Gills—the hardest worker on the team," Mr. Quinn said. "The one who never wants to get out of the water."

Mrs. Quinn handed Mom a ski. "You'll like this one, Carrie. It's nice and light."

The first time Mr. Quinn accelerated, Mom fell flat on her face. The second time, she pulled herself up, wavered, and tumbled into the water again. Mr. Quinn spun the boat in a circle back to the dock and his wife threw the rope to Mom.

"Third time's a charm!" she yelled.

Please get up, please get up, I chanted in my head. I tried to visualize Mom standing up on her ski, triumphant, showing them all how it was done.

It worked. This time, when the boat took off, Mom pulled herself up to a standing position. She leaned back and started to weave across the wake of the boat like Maddy's mom had done. The first couple passes were slow and unsteady, but with each one she gathered speed and leaned farther, sending walls of rainbow spray into the air.

It's funny how you can know someone your whole life and then out of nowhere they reveal some power you didn't know they had. Something that existed inside them all along, only they never had the chance to use it. My mom could ski like a superhero.

By the time we passed the public beach, she was sending rainbows shoulder-high in the air. She reached her arm down while she turned and touched the water with her hand. Then she skimmed off to the side again, pulled in the rope to gain momentum, and jumped right over the wake. She soared through the air for a split second, then her ski landed on the water with a slap.

We all clapped and screamed.

"Woo! Mom!" I yelled.

"You want to try it next, Anthoni?" Mr. Quinn shouted over the engine.

"No, thanks!" But in my head I could feel it—the wind in my hair, the pull of the rope on my arms, the speed, the adrenaline. I knew I could do it. I had good balance, and I was strong. As I watched Mom ski, Thunder Lake morphed in front of my eyes. Instead of a murky, threatening force, I saw powerful waves and rainbow mist.

Mom had tamed it, and it was making her stronger. I imagined myself jumping over the wake and sending a wall of spray into the sky like Storm summoning the rain.

As we neared the bay, I glanced at The Showboat Resort. From far away, the hotel looked clean and white. You couldn't see the cracked windows or the weeds. It almost looked as shiny and inviting as it did in the postcard. Mom geared up to do her jump again. This time she sailed higher in the air, but as she was coming down, Mr. Quinn swerved abruptly to the left. Instead of landing with a triumphant slap, Mom hit the water. Her ski flew into the air as she somersaulted and disappeared into Thunder Lake.

"Mom!" I yelled.

Mrs. Quinn poked her husband in the arm. "What was *that*?"

"Sorry," he said. "I thought . . . I saw something. I didn't want to hit it."

At first, I thought he was goofing around like before, but he didn't wink. His eyes were serious. The empty rope bounced wildly on the water as Mr. Quinn spun the boat around. I craned my neck and scanned the lake, but the boat's waves made the surface choppy and unclear. I couldn't see a thing.

17

SECRETS

Mom adjusted the ice pack on her face and took the glass of wine Mr. Quinn handed her.

"That's what I get for showing off," she said.

All the adults laughed as if my mom hadn't been seconds away from a trip to the emergency room on a gurney. From the boat, it had looked like she got clobbered with her ski, but she'd curled up in a ball to protect herself and bumped her knee into her cheekbone, barely missing her eye. Mr. Quinn had looked worried when he helped her into the boat, and Mrs. Quinn gave her a towel and rubbed her back while we motored slowly toward the house. After it turned out to be only a bruise, they all acted like it was hilarious.

"You've still got it, Gills," Mr. Quinn said. "The Somersault Crash—classic move!"

I didn't find it funny. Especially considering that it was his fault. Mom would have landed the jump fine if he hadn't swerved like a madman. Even Mrs. Quinn said he ought to have his eyes checked.

"I told you. I saw something." Mr. Quinn threw his hands in the air like a wanted criminal.

Mrs. Quinn rolled her eyes. "Sure. One of Maddy's mermaids?"

Mermaids? I tried to catch Maddy's eye but she was focused on her fork. I didn't get her. At the beach she was all look-at-me attitude, in the boat she was a laugh riot, but at home she was a mouse. She hadn't said a single word all through dinner.

The adults traded stories about what Eagle Waters was like when they were kids. Mom laughed a lot, and it struck me that she hadn't mentioned Beauty & the Bee all night. Not one word about eye shadow, or wrinkle cream, or the work-from-home opportunity of a lifetime. She didn't usually wait this long to start her pitch. She was probably angling for the right moment.

In the middle of the second story about Mr. Quinn's stunt as a human ski, Maddy set down her fork.

"Want to go to my room?" she asked.

Mom gave me an encouraging smile, and I followed Maddy upstairs.

We stood in front of the marshmallow bed and Maddy chewed her fingernail while I studied the mural on her wall. I thought through my usual list of conversation-starters.

"What would you rather have?" I asked. "Telepathy like Emma Frost or the ability to control weather like Storm?"

Maddy stopped chewing her fingernail. "You read X-Men?"

I nodded. "I'd rather have telepathy," I said. "Life would be a lot easier if you knew what everyone was thinking."

Maddy laughed. It was a nice laugh, like the laugh in the boat. Not the snarky laugh I'd heard at the beach.

"True," she said, "but I'd rather make storms."

She walked across the room and opened the door to her closet, closing it quickly behind her. When she came out, she was wearing her rectangular glasses. She tossed a stack of comics on the floor and sat down cross-legged.

"Start with this one," she said. She handed me a vintage *Uncanny X-Men* with a hologram of Magneto on the cover. "It's my favorite."

Then she smiled at me. A full-on, magical, let's-be-friends kind of smile.

I sat down on the floor next to her and opened the comic book. It was Magneto's origin story. Magneto was one of the most interesting X-Men because he could be very good or very evil, and you never knew which way he was going to go. Depending on which issues you'd read, it was easy to misjudge him. I supposed that was true with humans, too. Maddy, for instance.

I played around with the thought while I flipped the pages. If I'd learned anything from comics, it was that one small panel never gives you the whole story. It turned out the real Maddy Quinn wasn't the one I met on the beach at all. I bet she was sick that day, or her cat ran away, so she was feeling extra jealous, mean, and cranky, like when Magneto's daughter died and he lashed out and almost destroyed the world. Some people need a second chance. I let my mind take Maddy's smile and run with it, imagining the next few weeks—the two of us water-skiing together, having sleepovers, reading comics, and telling secrets.

"Want to know a secret?" Maddy asked.

My stomach flipped. Did she already *have* telepathy? Was that why she chose storms?

"I'm writing my own comic book. A series." That smile again.

"Really? About what?"

Maddy pushed her glasses up on her nose, and leaned forward. "A mermaid."

She slipped into her closet again, and when she returned, she handed me a full page from a comic that had been inked, colored, and lettered by hand.

"Here's a page I finished today."

Three small panels at the top of the page featured a beautiful mermaid with long, wavy hair, swimming happily toward an underwater city. In a much larger panel below, the mermaid looked straight ahead and opened her mouth to reveal huge fangs. Her eyes were narrow bloodred slits and her hair floated wildly around her head. The speech bubble read: *Ska-REEEEEEEEEEEEE!*

"Scary mermaid," I said.

"Thanks," Maddy said. "Her name's Lexie. She drinks blood and she has supersonic powers. She confuses her enemies with her beauty, then drags them down to her lair."

"It's really cool. Why's it a secret?"

Maddy shook her head. "People here think my drawings are weird," she said. "Even Julie. My teacher made me go to the school counselor because she said it's not normal for a girl to draw people getting their heads ripped off by a mermaid."

"That's terrible," I said. "They're not weird. They're awesome."

"It was different in Chicago, don't you think?"

I barely remembered Chicago, but I nodded anyway. I couldn't believe it. My Action Steps were practically completing themselves. Maddy and I had made a Meaningful Connection and I hadn't even tried. She liked me. We had things in common. We'd laughed, and now we were already at Step Three: Develop Trust—the most important step. I didn't want to screw it up. *Don't bee needy*, I reminded myself. *Find a way to bee needed.*

"I remember your grandpa," Maddy said. "He was hilarious. Is he still in Chicago?"

"Yeah," I said. "In a nursing home. But I haven't seen him for a while." A while. Saying it out loud made me realize how long it had been. Five years. I didn't even know what his room looked like.

Maddy looked sympathetic.

"My grandpa moved to New Mexico," she said. "When I was a kid, he used to tell the best stories. He had this one about a mermaid who lived in Thunder Lake . . ."

My mouth went dry. "A mermaid in Thunder Lake?"

"Yeah." Maddy rolled her eyes. "I totally believed it. When I first moved here, I used to make Julie go look for her with me. Anyway, that's where I got the idea. For Lexie."

The words were out of my mouth before I even knew they were coming.

"I've seen her," I blurted. "I've seen the mermaid."

The moment I said it, I knew it was true. In fact, I think I'd known it ever since I'd seen Charlotte Boulay dive in and not come up. The Boulay Mermaid photo looked too real to be a hoax.

Maddy blinked at me behind her glasses.

"I know it sounds impossible," I said. "It *is* impossible. She doesn't look . . . *anything* like what you'd think, but I swear . . ."

A slow smile spread across Maddy's face.

"For real?"

"For real."

Maddy's eyes got saucer-wide, and her grin sent goose bumps pricking down my spine.

"Maddy!" We both flinched as Mr. Quinn called up from downstairs. "Julie's on the phone."

"Tell her I'll call her later," she yelled.

"What am I? Your personal assistant? Tell her yourself."

Maddy shot me an apologetic look. I waved my hand.

"I'm cool here," I said, trying not to let on that I was doing cartwheels on the inside. This evening was going better than I could have dreamed. It was like I'd stepped through a doorway to an alternate universe where everything was brighter. More colorful. Filled with possibility. I couldn't stop smiling.

As I waited, I read the rest of the Magneto issue and took another look at the Lexie drawing. It really was good. The hair actually looked like it was floating in the water. I stood up and stretched my legs. In my mind, I checked off Action Step Three, and thought through the final two steps in my plan: Discover Her Secret Dream and Do What It Takes to make that dream come true.

I looked around the room. What was Maddy's secret dream? To be an artist? How could I help with that? I wondered how many more mermaid illustrations were in the closet. A comic book's worth? A whole series? If I saw them all, I could get an idea about what to do next. I touched the doorknob, but paused. I should wait for Maddy to show me.

Emma Frost stared at me from the other side of the room, as if she was sending me telepathic messages. Or trying to. What would Emma Frost do? There was zero chance she'd stand around second-guessing. She'd get the plan done. I only had a few weeks in Eagle Waters. The faster I could discover Maddy's secret dream, the faster I'd have a True Blue Friend for life—guaranteed!

I opened the door.

Maddy's closet was the size of a small bedroom and there wasn't one piece of clothing in it. There was a comfy chair, a lamp, two bookshelves, and a real artist's easel with organized cubbies for pens, pencils, and erasers. One bookshelf was full of comics, and the other held dozens of stuffed animals, mostly dolphins. I picked up an especially squishy dolphin. It had the softest fur I'd ever touched.

As I moved toward the easel, something glittery caught my eye. A pendant in the shape of a star hung from the lampshade. I turned on the lamp to get a better look. It was an old-fashioned hair clip tied to a string.

The silhouette of a mermaid balanced in the center of the star, and the way it dangled made the lamp cast a mermaid-shaped shadow on the wall. It looked familiar, but I couldn't remember why.

I heard footsteps on the stairs, and I quickly switched off the lamp. I told myself it was fine, I wasn't doing anything bad, but my hands shook as I tried to put the squishy dolphin back on the shelf. I knocked another one onto the floor, picked it up, knocked over a third, and before I knew what was happening, stuffed animals were tumbling to the ground. The footsteps were getting closer, almost outside Maddy's room. In a panic, I left the dolphins in a heap, shut the closet door, and threw myself onto the floor in front of Maddy's marshmallow bed.

I opened a comic book to a random page and tried to breathe like a person who wasn't doing anything but sitting around reading about Magneto. And then I saw it: a fuzzy, pale-blue dolphin the size of my fist lay on the carpet in front of the closet door. It must have tumbled out in the avalanche. I lunged for it, but before I could find a place to put it, the doorknob turned.

I shoved the dolphin under my shirt and crossed my arms over my belly to cover up the bulge.

"Sorry about that," Maddy said as she walked into the room. "Julie's a motormouth. I hope I never get poison ivy. It sounds disgusting." She adjusted her glasses and looked at me. "You okay?"

My heart was pounding so loudly, I was certain she could hear it. I forced a smile.

"Fine," I said.

"Your face is really red."

Of course it was. I had a stuffed dolphin under my shirt and no idea what to do with it. I thought about confessing, but how was that going to sound? *Hey, Maddy, I snooped in your closet, knocked your toys on the ground, and rubbed one of them all over my belly button.* So much for Developing Trust.

"Your mom said you have to go now. I'll see you at swim lessons?"

"Okay."

"I want to know more about . . . you-know-who." She dropped her voice to a whisper. "It'll be our secret."

Maddy Quinn and I had a secret.

We grinned at each other until it finally sunk into my thick brain that I was supposed to get up off the floor and leave. With a stuffed sea creature stowed away in my shirt.

Miserably, I gripped the squishy lump with one hand and pushed myself up off the floor with the other.

"You sure you're feeling okay?" Maddy asked.

"Stomachache," I mumbled, holding the dolphin close to my belly.

And then—I could hardly believe it—Maddy linked her arm through mine as we walked down the stairs. Even as I clutched the smuggled dolphin, happy thoughts ricocheted through my mind. In a tiny, run-down town in the middle of nowhere with nothing to do but swat mosquitoes, I had found a friend. Not just any friend. A friend who could trick ski and illustrate beautiful, terrifying mermaids. A friend who liked X-Men and trusted me with secrets.

And now I was going to steal her dolphin?

The hopeful feeling disintegrated. I paused at the bottom of the stairs, reached under my shirt, and held out the fuzzy bottlenose. Maddy dropped my arm.

I stammered, "I didn't mean to . . . I thought . . . your drawings were really cool . . ."

Maddy's mouth puckered up like she'd eaten something sour. In the middle of my apology, she snatched the dolphin out of my hand and ran upstairs to her room.

18

NOVELTY ACTS OF THE VAUDEVILLE STAGE

W ant to watch a movie?" Mom settled onto the couch and put her feet up on the wicker coffee table. It had started to rain, and the cabin was filled with the patter of raindrops on the roof. It almost felt cozy.

I did want to watch a movie. It might take my mind off Maddy Quinn. The whole drive home, I kept imagining her opening her closet door, seeing the avalanche of stuffed dolphins, and letting out a loud *Ska-REEEEEEE!* It didn't help that Mom couldn't shut up about Maddy's X-Men mural and how much we had in common and how it was like I'd manifested the perfect True Blue Friend by thinking positive thoughts and wasn't it all just Meant to Be.

"Earth to Anthoni," Mom said. "You okay?"

Mom wouldn't understand about snooping around in Maddy's room. Snooping wasn't the kind of activity that attracted positive results. So I had to ask carefully.

"Did you ever do something sort of bad, but not that bad, and then make it worse by trying to fix it, but in a really dumb way that turns out terribly, and then your friend wouldn't forgive you for it?"

Mom raised her eyebrows. "That's pretty specific," she said. "And vague. Can I get more details? Gillis Girls Tell Each Other Everything, right?"

I raised an eyebrow at her. "We used to."

Mom looked hurt, and even though it wasn't my fault that what I'd said was true, I regretted saying it. And I didn't want to talk about Queen Bee again. Not now. I had bigger problems.

"I think I messed things up with Maddy," I said.

Mom waited, and when I didn't offer more, she nodded thoughtfully. "I've done something like that," she said. "Usually the best thing to do is to say you're sorry and really mean it. A True Blue Friend will forgive you eventually."

I sighed. Maddy Quinn wasn't my True Blue Friend yet. I was right there at Action Step Three: Develop Trust, and I'd blown it. For what? Sure, I'd seen Maddy's secret studio, so maybe technically I'd made it all the way to Action Step Four: Discover Her Secret Dream. But if Maddy wanted to be a comic-book artist, I couldn't think of a single way to help.

I listened to the rain and imagined it splashing into Thunder Lake, each drop sending out a small circle of ripples—hundreds of tiny clones of the splash that Charlotte made every morning when she dove into Thunder Lake. I sat up straighter. The mermaid splash. Maddy's eyes had lit up when I'd mentioned the mermaid. What if seeing a real live mermaid was her secret dream? If that was true, this dolphin thing was only a small setback. A detour. I couldn't help Maddy become an artist, but I could show her a mermaid.

I looked sideways at Mom. She was scrolling through movie options on her phone.

I tried to make my voice sound casual, like chitchat. "Did you ever hear of the Boulay Mermaid?"

"The what?" Mom's thumbs continued to scroll.

"Boulay Mermaid," I said.

"Actually, yeah." She looked up at the ceiling like she was trying to remember something stuck far back in her brain. "I forgot about that. Mr. Boulay used to claim he had mermaids in the family."

"He did?"

Mom rolled her eyes. "He was always telling stories to get the ski team riled up. He had half of us convinced there was a family of foxes living on the second floor of the hotel. Why? How'd you hear about it?"

That was a tough one. If snooping wasn't a positive-result activity, breaking into The Black Bear, pawing through someone else's closet, and "borrowing" a secret photo was downright negative. Not only was I *not* going to tell Mom everything, I needed to tell a white lie.

"I brought Charlotte Boulay a Wrinkle-Free sample and she told me about it."

Mom put down the phone and gave me an odd look. "That was thoughtful of you," she said. "Every time I try to go over there, she seems to disappear. But . . . next time, you shouldn't visit her alone. I'm sure she's very nice, but she *is* a little eccentric."

"Do you think it's real?" I asked.

"Sure. The key to the Wrinkle-Free line is to use it regularly. If you don't apply it every morning and night . . ."

"I mean the Boulay Mermaid. Do you think it could be real?"

Mom laughed. "If Charlotte Boulay told you she's a mermaid, I think the choking heron was a more believable act."

"I'm serious."

"She was pulling your leg, sweetie. Clearly, that's her thing."

I felt an inexplicable lump in my throat. I didn't exactly

expect her to jump on board, but I thought she'd at least give the idea a chance.

"Gramps tried for a year straight to get you to believe in fairies," she said. "Are you saying he should have tried mermaids?"

I didn't laugh. I always *wanted* to believe in fairies, but I couldn't because they weren't real. If Gramps had shown me photographic evidence and firsthand witness experience? I might have thought he was on to something.

Mom reached for her phone. "Okay. We can look it up."

I leaned close to her while she typed in "Boulay Mermaid." Not much came up—a list of entertainers at The Palace in 1934, a short story that contained the phrase "Dr. Boulay's mermaid obsession," and an article titled "Novelty Acts of the Vaudeville Stage."

"That makes sense," Mom said. She clicked on the link. "Mr. Boulay used to be a vaudeville actor."

"Vaudeville?"

"It was kind of an old-timey variety show," she said. "Dancing, singing, comedy acts, magic. It used to be popular, especially before movies were invented. I think the 'novelty acts' were more gimmicky . . . well, like these, for instance."

The article contained short descriptions of novelty acts like Willard, the Man Who Grows, who could add seven and a half inches to his height; and Dave Monihan, who played xylophone with his feet. Halfway down the page was an entry for the Boulay Mermaid:

THE BOULAY MERMAID, 1933–1942. Developed by Frank and Selina Boulay, a moderately popular explorer act known for presenting "curiosities" from around the world. Early acts included a dragon's egg, a boxing kangaroo, and a talking dog that spoke only Hungarian. Their most popular act began in 1933 when the Boulays claimed to have adopted a mermaid girl from the South Seas. The Boulay Mermaid sang and performed onstage in a large glass water tank and was a repeat act at The Palace Theatre in its final year of operation. In 1940, the Boulays moved the act to a resort town in Wisconsin. The show was so realistic that many visitors claimed to believe an actual mermaid did live in the flesh at The Showboat Resort.

"The Palace Theatre," Mom said, impressed. "That was a big deal. So . . . real, but not real. There's your answer."

"It doesn't exactly say it's fake," I said, though I knew it sounded ridiculous.

"You're right," Mom said. "And I think we should get one of those talking Hungarian dogs. I've always wanted one."

I stuck my tongue out at her, but I couldn't help smiling.

"Thanks for looking it up," I said.

Mom put her arm around me and I leaned my head on her chest. Her hair smelled like honey. I let my eyes close and my body relax.

"Speaking of Charlotte Boulay," she said. "I ought to call some clients. Why don't you put on a movie, and I'll get some work done?"

"Noooo," I said. "What about your face? You should rest. Please?" I *wanted* her to work so we could sign up Worker Bees and get our lives back on track, but I also didn't want to move. I hadn't forgiven her for messing things up, but it felt nice to lie there, feeling the rise and fall of her chest under my head.

Mom stood up.

"I'll make my calls in the back room," she said. "Here, I know exactly what you should watch."

She put on an old movie called *Splash* about a boy who meets a mermaid and later in life, the mermaid comes to New York City to find him. It was funny, but watching a movie by yourself is lonely. And it did nothing to help me stop thinking about Maddy or Charlotte Boulay.

The more I thought about it, I had to admit that the vaudeville act explanation made sense. Sure, the costume in Charlotte's picture had looked real, but the mermaid tail in *Splash* looked at least as good. As for the dive, maybe I'd fallen asleep before Charlotte resurfaced, or maybe I dreamed the whole thing. I felt silly. Mom was right. I'd never been one of those kids who fell easily for things like fairies and unicorns. I should have known better.

In the movie, the bad guy discovered the mermaid and was whisking her off to his science lab to study her, but my eyelids kept closing. The movie music started to meld with the sound of Mom's phone calls in the back room, and as I drifted off to sleep, one last, awful thought swam through my mind.

If Charlotte Boulay wasn't a mermaid, how was I going to win back Maddy Quinn?

19

SPLASH! TAKE TWO

*B*e *my friend! Be my friend!"*

I shook the mermaid's shoulders, but she squinted her eyes and showed me her silver fangs. I shook her harder and yelled again, "Be my friend!"

The mermaid's head morphed into the head of Charlotte Boulay. "You like that?" she cackled. "I got a million of 'em."

I screamed.

The mermaid yanked out of my grasp, and her head morphed again. Maddy Quinn floated in front of me. Her arms were full of stuffed dolphins, and she glared at me as she opened her mouth: Ska-REEEEEEEEEEE!

* * *

I jerked awake.

My heart was going a mile a minute. I felt a soft blanket over me, and took in the dusty smell of the couch.

I wasn't underwater.

I sat up and listened to the rain on the roof of The Blue Heron.

My head had *not* been ripped off by a morphing, bloodthirsty mermaid.

I wrapped the blanket around my shoulders and climbed the ladder to the loft. The rungs creaked underneath my feet.

It was too early to be up, but thanks to my nightmare, I was wide-awake. So instead of falling into bed, I sat on the window seat and watched the clouds change from gray-blue to yellow-pink over Thunder Lake. The rain was letting up, and a soft breeze blew in from the window. A loon let out a lonely wail. I cringed, but steadied myself. I wasn't falling for that one again.

As the sun peeked over the trees and shot a hazy orange glow into the clouds, I heard footsteps on the dock below my window. Charlotte Boulay's orange hair caught the light, and I watched her walk to the edge of the dock. She paused, adjusted her bright-pink swimsuit, and looked up at the sky. A few scattered raindrops sent ripples circling on the surface of the lake.

Charlotte raised her arms and dove.

When she didn't come up, I scanned the shore,

looking for a logical explanation—she could hold her breath a long time, or had trained herself to swim long distances underwater. Or she'd already come up for air, and I wasn't looking in the right place.

After a few minutes, there was a splash toward the edge of the bay, where Mom had tumbled out of her ski. I leaned against the window and squinted. There was something on the water, but it could be anything. A loon, a duck, a floating stick.

Quickly, I climbed down the ladder of the loft and grabbed Mom's phone from the charger in the kitchen. The camera lens could zoom. It might not be far enough, but it would be better than nothing.

By the time I got back to the window seat, the water was as still as glass. I was too late. I wrapped the blanket back around me and used the camera lens to zoom in on the squirrel nest instead. What a mess.

Another small splash came from farther away, near the edge of the bay. I focused the camera. There was a person out there, head bobbing above the surface. As I watched, the head disappeared into the water again but came back up in the same spot. Down. Then up. What was she doing?

The fourth time, she stayed down. I started to believe she'd vanished for good, but then I heard a splash, and she appeared in front of the dock. She pulled herself up with surprising arm strength and sat on the edge, dangling her feet in the water. I zoomed the camera in on her legs. They looked normal. No scales, not one sign of a tail. Clearly, it was proof that, like fairies, mermaids don't exist and only a three-year-old would believe otherwise. So why was there still a nagging voice in the back of my head whispering: *Maybe?*

As I zoomed the camera out, I saw something else. Her wet head was bent, forehead in her hands, and her shoulders were bobbing up and down. Charlotte Boulay was crying.

20
TEAM GOALS

Mom gave me a pleading look and pointed to the coffeepot. She was on a video call with her Worker Bees, but it wasn't going well. I refilled her cup as one of the pixilated women on the screen jerked from pose to pose like a robot as she talked.

"Kimmy," Mom said loudly. She studied a chart in her binder and marked it with a highlighter. "If you're going to place that order anyway, can you get it in before the end of the week? Kimmy? You're freezing up again."

I poured myself a bowl of cereal and shook it in front of Mom's face to see if she wanted any. She shooed me away and tried to keep her voice cheerful.

"Sara, are *you* still there? Bee's Knees is the free gift for the month of June—but tell your client she can have two free gifts if she gets a friend to order, too. But it has to be this week. Sara? Sara? Can you hear me?"

I chewed my cereal and watched Mom frown into the camera. It used to be that her end-of-month conference calls were all about who won the bonus movie tickets and spa coupons that Mom bought for her top sellers. It was like a party online, with all the Worker Bees cheering, and Mom congratulating them like they'd won a million dollars. But over the past year, she had stopped announcing prizes and spent more time talking about strategies to get the most out of the last few days of the month. Now she looked pained. There was no way she was going to motivate her team with a negative attitude. Mom needed to Change Her State.

I made a monkey face at her, and she smiled a little, so I did a robot dance in my chair to make her laugh. She needed to pep up and put on a bit of the old Chief Pollinator charm.

"Girls, hold on a minute." Mom lowered her laptop screen. "You're really distracting me," she whispered. "Go play outside."

"Fine. In a minute."

To get my mind off the depressing call, I read Mom's whiteboard as I slurped down the rest of my cereal. I almost choked on the last bite. On the GOAL section of her board, Mom had added *Pay Off Credit Card* underneath *Rent: Mr. Li*. She'd never told me anything about a credit card. How much did we owe on that? The month-end bonus was only going to be enough to cover Mr. Li. What happens if you don't pay your credit card? Would we get dragged deeper and deeper into debt until . . . what? Until we had to live in the Beemobile? I knew a kid in Ann Arbor who lived in his station wagon. It wasn't out of the question.

Before I left the cabin, I dropped a note onto Mom's keyboard: *Negative Thoughts Attract Negative Results.* Then I headed to The Black Bear to look for my backpack.

The wooden bear cub was dark and damp from the rain. I high-fived him before I hopped onto the porch and jiggled the screen door handle. The handle clicked, and I pulled it open, feeling around for the key to the inside door, but it wasn't there. I bumped the door with my knee and it creaked open.

"Hi-YAAAA!"

I stumbled backward and fell flat on my butt on the front porch. I scrambled to get up, prepared to run for The Blue Heron as fast as my legs could take me, but then I saw DJ flinging his limbs around in a flurry of fake karate moves. When he realized it was me, he dropped his arms.

"Oh, hi, Gills. I thought you might be a ghost or something."

"And flailing around like a madman would scare a ghost?"

"It's worth a shot."

I held back seven cranky comments and dusted myself off. DJ went back to sorting his rocks. He was in the process of moving the entire collection from the bedroom to the kitchen counter, table, and shelves.

"It's easier to sort them in here," he explained. "Now that it doesn't smell so bad."

I picked up a pink-colored rock with a tiny purple stripe.

DJ took it out of my hand and set it back on the table. "That's Baraboo Quartzite," he said. "It's metamorphic."

"Like Mystique?"

"What?"

"Mystique. From X-Men. She can psionically shift the atoms in her body to morph into anyone she wants."

DJ shrugged. "I've never seen those movies."

"They were comics first," I said. If Maddy had been there, she would have set him straight.

"This is my best one." He reached into his pocket and took out another pink rock. "My parents and I found it camping at Devil's Lake," he said. "It's ancient. Thousands of millions of years old. See these ripples?"

He handed me the rock. It was a deep maroon color with a jagged edge and five dark-purple bands. It was beautiful. One section did look wavy, like the ripples near the dock after Charlotte Boulay dove in.

"The ripple shows it used to be underwater sandstone, which isn't very strong, but the glaciers put so much pressure on it that the grains of sand cemented together and morphed into quartzite. It's so tough and durable that in the Stone Age, it was used to make tools like axes and stone-hammers."

I ran my thumb along the jagged edge. It was sharp. I could imagine an early human using it to chop kindling for a fire.

"Baraboo Quartzite has iron fused into it, too—that's why it's purple."

"So it's more like Wolverine," I said.

"Who?"

"You've got to be kidding me." Did the kid live in a hole? "Wolverine. From the X-Men. Scientists wanted to use him as a weapon, so they fused his bones with metal."

"I guess." DJ took the quartzite from my hand and put it back in his pocket. "My dad said I should carry it for good luck, but it doesn't really work."

"So why do you carry it?"

"Same as ghost karate," he said. "It's worth a shot."

"Good luck with that."

I headed to the bedroom.

"Hey, DJ," I yelled. "Where'd you put my backpack?"

"I thought you took it," he called back.

"I left it on the bed, but it's not here."

I heard rocks clattering, and DJ met me in the doorway. His eyebrows lifted to the ceiling, and he let air whistle through his teeth.

"Don't mess with me," I said. "Where is it? I need it."

"I'm not kidding you, Gills. I haven't seen it."

We checked everywhere—under the bed, in the closet, the living room, kitchen, even the bathroom and the loft.

"Do you think a ghost took it?" DJ asked.

I sat down at the picnic table in the kitchen. Two small rainbows of light danced above DJ's rocks. I looked up at the window where two butterfly sun catchers dangled above the sink.

"Did you put those there?" I asked, pointing to the window.

DJ shook his head.

"They weren't there before?"

DJ's nostrils flared. "No!"

I had a weird feeling like someone was watching me from behind. I turned around slowly, but no one was there.

"Okay, then. Will you come with me?" I asked.

"Where?"

"The Showboat. I think Charlotte Boulay has my backpack."

DJ gaped at me. "What are you going to do? Just ask her for it?"

"Yup."

"For someone who's afraid of the water, you're pretty brave," he said.

"I'm not afraid of the water. Look, you said you wanted to see her. Are you in or out?"

I tried to look like I didn't care, but I hoped he was in. Mom had asked me not to go see Charlotte alone. I wasn't sure a strange, rock-obsessed boy with ghost-karate skills was going to meet her security standards, but it was better than nothing. Besides, the last time I'd seen Charlotte Boulay, she was crying her eyes out on the dock, and the time before that, she'd disappeared in the dark. I had no idea what I was walking into.

DJ hesitated, then scrunched his face into a tight grimace and let loose a loud, quick "AHHH!" like he'd been stabbed in the gut.

"Are you all right?"

He shook out his shoulders and arms and pumped his legs in place.

"Okay," he said. "I'm ready. But if I yell 'Gonzo!' that's when we run."

21

THE WEIGHT OF
THE PAST

Charlotte Boulay stood on the lawn of the Show-boat hotel and waved a feather duster at us.

DJ slowed his steps. "She knows," he whispered. "She knows we broke into her cabin and puked on her floor."

"She doesn't know we puked," I said, pulling him up the path by his shirtsleeve.

"What's she doing?"

It was a good question. The lawn outside the hotel was strewn with empty cardboard boxes. Charlotte traipsed around them in a maid's uniform—only instead of a plain white apron, hers was covered with bright pink and blue butterflies. Her hair was wrapped in a matching butterfly maid's cap.

As we got closer, we could hear old-timey music

streaming from the windows of the hotel. Charlotte weaved her body around the boxes, swaying her hips, and occasionally kicking a foot in the air. Messy stacks of picture frames were piled on the grass around her. She leaned over, picked one up, and gave her feather duster an artistic flourish. She wasn't exactly cleaning, and she wasn't exactly dancing either.

"If it isn't my busy bees," she said in a Southern drawl. "Y'all do inspiring work. That was one ship-shape clean job." She smoothed her apron and tiptoed toward us, extending a gloved hand to DJ. "Dana Johnson, I presume. I don't believe we've met," she drawled. *Formally.*"

DJ flinched and poked my ribs with his cast, about three times harder than necessary.

"Ow!"

"How does she know who I am?" he hissed through his teeth.

"Shhh!" I elbowed him back.

Charlotte pretended not to hear any of it. She stood there with her hand extended until, finally, DJ reached his good arm forward.

"People call me DJ," he mumbled.

But before he could shake her hand, Charlotte whipped a mini feather duster out of the pocket of her apron and placed it in his outstretched palm.

"Now, aren't you a gallant fella?" she said. "Yes, of *course*, I'd love some help." She gestured to the picture frames lying in the grass. "Dust 'em down, stick 'em in a box. Easy as pe-can pie."

DJ's mouth dropped open and he looked at me for our next move. As if I had any clue.

"We came to see if the hotel has a Lost and Found," I said. "I misplaced my backpack."

"Yes. You did, didn't you?"

DJ elbowed me again, and I felt my cheeks get hot. *You did, didn't you?* What was that supposed to mean? Did she know where it was? Did she have it? I needed that backpack.

Charlotte Boulay produced another feather duster from her apron pocket and tossed it to me. I had two choices—catch it or let it fall to the ground. I caught it.

"Don't be shy now. I *know* you two can clean."

She picked a frame off the ground and handed it to DJ.

"What is it? A fire-dog?" he asked.

The frame held a photo of a dog balanced on the top of a ladder with a fire hose in his mouth and a tiny fire-man's hat perched on top of his head.

"Lord a'mercy," Charlotte said, keeping up the Southern accent. "*Never* agree to perform after an animal act. It's murder."

DJ kneeled down. He set the dog photo aside and picked up a picture of seven girls in feather tutus. Grass and dirt stuck to the back of the frame.

"Sister acts!" Charlotte huffed. "How saccharine can you get?"

"What is this stuff?" DJ asked. "It's freaky." He handed me a photo of a guy in a frog suit with his legs wrapped all the way around his shoulders.

"Hm. I once fell in love with a contortionist . . ." Charlotte's voice trailed away and she lifted her eyes to the sky in a thoughtful pose.

As I looked at the photo, an ant walked across the frame and marched onto my thumb.

I was getting annoyed. Not only was Charlotte ignoring my question about the backpack, her system made no sense. If she was going to dust off and box up a bunch of old photos, why bring them outside and get them dirtier than they already were?

"Why aren't you doing this inside?" I asked.

Charlotte reached her arms out and made a dramatic gesture toward the world around her—the sun, the blue sky, and Thunder Lake sparkling through the trees. "Look around you. It's a beautiful day. Any more questions?"

"Yes. My backpack?" I repeated. "Have you seen it?"

"Ahem!" Charlotte cleared her throat and the Southern accent came out thick and strong. "Ahm cleanin' house today. Gettin' rid of the riffraff. Clutter. Bric-a-brac. Help or scram, your choice."

DJ picked up another picture, balanced it on his cast,

and started dusting it. "It could be okay," he whispered to me. "This stuff is cool."

"Let me see that," I said, grabbing the photo. It was Lady Alice and her Dirty Rats. I don't know why, but it annoyed me even more, seeing her get shoved away in a box. I waved the frame at Charlotte Boulay.

"Why are you taking these down?" I asked.

Charlotte laid the back of her hand on her forehead like she could just wilt. She held the pose, then shouted at the top of her lungs, "Oh my heavens, the *weight* of the past!"

DJ looked alarmed.

Charlotte straightened her dress and stared me in the eye. "I've been drowning in the past my whole life," she said, dropping the Southern accent. "I'm tired of being reminded. The past is past. It's time to let go."

A new song began to pour out of the windows of The Showboat, and Charlotte tiptoed around again, waving her feather duster in the air like a woman doing a scarf dance. She sang along to the music in a pinched, nasal voice.

"Laugh, laugh, and the world laughs with you . . ."

Then she whirled back around to face us, put her face in her hands and dragged her eyelids down like a zombie.

"Cry, cry, and you cry alone," she growled in a low, gravelly man's voice.

She went back on her tiptoes. "No, no, laugh!" the nasal woman said in a scolding, horrified tone.

"Cry, cry, cry!" the zombie man growled.

It was possibly the weirdest thing I'd ever seen. As she went from high to low, she contorted her body and her voice so much that I almost forgot it was Charlotte Boulay standing in front of us.

A snort came out of DJ's nose. He started to giggle, which only egged Charlotte on. Her characters fought harder and faster, and soon, the tiptoed woman appeared to get confused.

"Cry! No! Laugh! Cry!" the high-pitched voice stumbled. Then she squealed, "Oooh, you big lout!" and she smacked herself on the butt with her duster.

DJ lost it. He dropped to his knees, laughing helplessly, and even though I was frustrated with Charlotte Boulay, I lost it, too. We sat on the weedy lawn in front of the boat-shaped hotel and laughed our heads off. The whole thing was so bizarre that there wasn't anything else you *could* do.

Charlotte curtsied and grinned. "Like that?" she said. "I got a million of 'em." Then she motioned to the photos. "Chop-chop. These memories aren't going to box themselves."

We boxed picture frame after picture frame, and every time I thought we were done, Charlotte would go back into The Showboat and come out with more. She didn't do much packing. Mostly, she flitted about, dancing, peering over our shoulders, and answering DJ's nonstop questions.

"Did you know all these people? Are they your friends?"

"Sure. Best friends for a week. Till they moved on to their next gig, and I never saw them again. Believe me, everyone says they'll visit and write, but no one ever does." She shot me a knowing glance. "Do they, Anthoni?"

Of course they didn't, but how did she know *I* knew about that?

"Did you know Houdini?" DJ asked, holding up a photo of a man with thick chains wound around his neck and arms.

She leaned in confidentially. "He kissed his wife goodbye before each stunt, and she passed him the key mouth-to-mouth. That's how he made his escape."

"Gross. Why does this one say, 'See you in jail, Frankie Boy'?"

Charlotte paused. "Well," she said, finally. "My father spent a lot of time there."

DJ and I glanced at each other.

"Visiting?" he asked, hopefully.

"No, locked up."

I hadn't thought about it before—bank robbers and murderers had kids, too.

"What'd he do?" I asked, though I wasn't sure I wanted to know.

Charlotte let us stew in silence. Then she laughed. "You two look like I'm going to eat you up! You really want the whole, dastardly tale?"

We nodded.

"Suit yourself. When I was a kid, my folks and I were on the circuit. We performed in a different town every week, sometimes four or five shows a day. It was a good gig, but some lawyer decided I was too young to work that hard and called it 'cruelty to children.' So after every show, my dad either got fined or arrested. That's all."

"If it was against the law, why did he make you do it?" I asked.

"Yeah," DJ said. "Why didn't you quit?"

"And give up showbiz? A Boulay? Never!" she said. "My folks would have sold me to pirates before giving up their gig. Besides, my act was hot. It was cheaper to pay the fine or spend the night in jail than to lose the income." Her voice still sounded like she was telling a funny story, but her smile had disappeared. She let out a short, sharp laugh and said, "It's the Boulay way—we'll risk anything for a quick buck and some cheap applause."

I closed up the last box, and Charlotte stared at it for a long moment. Then she clapped her hands together like she was bringing herself to attention. She spun around in a circle. Looking pleased, she reached out, grabbed my arm, and spun me in a circle, too. She spun me again and again, until everything whizzed by in a blur. The trees blended into one green smear, and I felt my hair flying weightless behind me. Even after she let go, I kept turning until DJ grabbed my shoulders and dared me to walk a straight line. I managed three steps before I stumbled and fell to the ground, laughing and light-headed, the world still spinning behind my eyes.

"How about a break?" Charlotte said. "Lemonade and ice-cream sundaes sound grand, don't they?"

22

ALL IS CHANGE

Charlotte Boulay placed a pink flowered tea set on the table and poured us each a cup of steaming black tea.

"Crackers, anyone?" she asked.

I bit into a stale saltine. DJ looked like he'd been robbed.

"So sue me," Charlotte said. "I said lemonade and sundaes *sounded* good. I didn't say I *had* any. Oh, sugar!" She snapped her fingers and disappeared into the kitchen.

DJ picked his teacup up by its dainty handle and sniffed. He put it back down, and tea sloshed over the rim into the saucer.

"Do you think it's safe to drink?" he asked.

Charlotte hummed as she came out of the kitchen. She set a tiny bowl of sugar cubes in front of us. "One lump or two?"

"Four, please," DJ said.

We'd left the boxes on the lawn and followed Charlotte into the front office. I hardly recognized it without all the photos. Hundreds of nails dotted the walls where the picture frames had been. The room felt bigger without all the clutter, but the blank white walls made it seem even more deserted. The mermaid lamp seemed to slouch by the bookshelf, and the traveling-trunk desk shrank into the back corner. Charlotte didn't appear to notice. She walked straight to the mermaid lamp and pushed against the bookshelf behind it. Silently, the wall shifted, and the bookshelf swung into the interior of the hotel.

"No way!" DJ said. "I always wanted to see one of those."

Charlotte winked at me.

"Is that how you sneak in and out?" I asked.

"You didn't think I could walk through walls, did you?"

We followed her through the secret doorway and up a few steps into the hotel lounge. The porthole windows all around the room made you feel like you were in the hull of a ship. They were positioned high enough so you couldn't see the grass outside at all—only a few trees, and beyond that, Thunder Lake. To add to the illusion, a big wooden steering wheel sat in the center of the room. You could almost convince yourself to be seasick.

The lounge was fancy in an old-fashioned, abandoned sort of way. Part of the room was lined with half-moon booths with thick, cushioned seats. DJ and I sunk into the cushions of the center booth while the tea steamed on the table in front of us. All the booths faced a giant stage and a tiki bar like you see in commercials for Hawaiian vacations. Above the stage was a large wooden plaque that read *The Showboat Lounge: Palace Theatre of the Wilderness!*

"Now then," Charlotte said. She scooted into our booth, sandwiching DJ in the center, and took a sip of her tea. "Let's talk turkey."

She reached under the booth and pulled out my backpack. DJ flinched and spilled his tea again. His cup was half empty, and he hadn't even taken one sip.

"I can explain," I said, but Charlotte held up a hand.

"Drink your tea. I'll do the talking."

DJ leaned toward me and whispered, "It's probably okay. She's drinking it, and hers is from the same pot."

Charlotte peered down her nose at him. "If you watched more movies, young man, you'd know that I could easily have spent decades building up an immunity to an arsenal of poisons before you were even born." Her mouth twitched into a smile. "But you're right. It's safe. See?" She took another sip.

DJ looked terrified. He kicked me under the table, and in case I didn't get the message, mouthed the words "Don't drink it."

Charlotte ignored him. "The facts are these: My trash collector informed me that the tin outside The Black Bear was full this week. I told him that was unlikely, but he was able to provide evidence in the mundane form of garbage, et cetera, et cetera, and here . . . we . . . are."

To punctuate her last words, she unzipped my backpack, reached her arm in, and took out the picture of the Boulay Mermaid.

"Most people," she continued, "don't approve of breaking into cabins and stealing personal property."

"I only wanted to borrow it," I said. "I wasn't going to steal it."

Charlotte held up her hand to shush me, but her fingers trembled. Her eyes were on the photo.

"You are obviously not hooligans," she said quietly, still studying the happy family in the frame. "In fact, The Black Bear was in need of a deep cleanse. So let's not cry over spilt milk."

She placed the photo face-down on the table next to the teapot and straightened her shoulders. "*Who* is the rock collector?"

DJ raised his hand tentatively. His face was fire-engine red. I was afraid if this went on much longer, his whole scalp might burst into flames.

"You may continue to house your collection in my cabin. Rent-free," she said. "My father was a collector of sorts.

"And you." She raised her cup in my direction and took another sip before reaching back into my backpack. She removed one of Josh's SpongeBob floaties and raised one eyebrow as she held it in the air. I winced. Next, she took out my notebook.

"That's mine!" I said. "It's private!"

Charlotte arched her eyebrow higher. "So is my cabin. You look through my things, I look through yours. Seems fair." She flipped through the pages. "Potentials . . . criteria . . . ah, this is the page."

She paused at *TRUE BLUE FRIEND: ACTION STEPS.*

I lunged for the notebook, but Charlotte whisked it out of my reach.

"I think you should know," she said, tapping her finger on the page, "that there is no such thing. And even if there was, this is *not* the way to do it."

"Do what?" DJ asked.

"Nothing," I said, and turned to Charlotte. "Put it away. Please?"

Charlotte considered the matter, then turned to DJ. "What I am trying to explain to your companion is that there is no such thing as a True Blue Friend."

I bit the inside of my cheek until it hurt.

"Oh, maybe for an hour, a day, a month," she continued. "But people change. They look out for themselves. Even the ones who love you most will turn on you in a dark moment. Worse yet, you'll turn on them."

"That's not true," I said. I tugged at DJ's arm. "We should go."

"I'm not being an ogre. I'm simply trying to save you some heartache."

Charlotte rested her hand on the photo of the Boulay Mermaid. Slowly, as if it were made of lead, she turned it over again.

"I haven't seen this photo in years. My mother should have been in the movies, don't you think?"

DJ shifted to get a closer look and knocked the teapot over with his cast. Charlotte let out a yelp and, with surprisingly quick reflexes, lifted the picture before it got wet. She shoved it into my hands. "Hold this," she said, and began sopping up the tea with her napkin.

"Sorry," DJ said in a pitiful voice. He reached across the table with his own napkin, and tipped over Charlotte's teacup, adding to the flood.

She ran to the kitchen to get a towel.

"Want to help?" DJ asked. He frantically wiped at the table with his sopping wet napkin. His entire neck was red now, and he gritted his teeth like he was in misery.

"Just a minute." Something in the photo had caught my eye. It was the star-shaped barrette holding back the

Boulay Mermaid's bangs. A mermaid silhouette was set in the center of the star.

When Charlotte returned with dishtowels, I held up the picture.

"I've seen this before."

"Obviously," she said. She handed DJ a towel and motioned to the growing puddle on the floor.

DJ crawled dutifully under the table to clean up the tea.

"Not the picture," I said. "The hair clip. A friend of mine has one exactly like it."

Charlotte froze for a second, then started stacking the teacups on a tray. "Impossible," she said. "My mother had that hairpin made—it's one of a kind."

DJ poked at my leg under the table.

"What happened to it, then?" I asked.

Charlotte turned toward the porthole windows and gazed out at Thunder Lake. The rims of her eyelids were red. "I was a foolish child," she said. "I threw it away in a dark moment. It's one of my deepest regrets."

DJ poked me again, and I shifted my leg away from him.

"Is that why you were crying?" I asked.

Charlotte set down a teacup and locked her blue eyes on mine.

"I saw you swimming this morning," I said. "Out in the bay. You were crying."

Charlotte's eyes narrowed. "Oh," she said. "Really?"

"Anthoni," DJ said from under the table, but I kept watching Charlotte Boulay. The image of Maddy's blood-thirsty mermaid popped into my mind. I wanted to look away, to break the stare, but I couldn't.

"You can stay underwater a long time," I said. "How do you do that?"

"Magic," she said flippantly.

"For real."

"I've got gills."

I held my breath. Was she being serious?

Twice, Charlotte opened her mouth and closed it. Then she shrugged and said, "Look, kid. What do you want to hear? Breathing tubes?"

DJ shook my leg hard. "GONZO!"

"*What*-zo?" Charlotte asked.

"DJ!" I said, and peered under the table.

"Anthoni," he whimpered. "I'm stuck."

23

SWIM LESSONS: TAKE TWO

"Okay, Anthoni," Mom said. "You've set your goal. Now visualize yourself achieving it."

I scanned the beach to see if anyone was looking at us. The sparkly-suit sunbathers were stretched out on their towels, parents and toddlers were busy with their sandcastles, and everyone else was preoccupied with another epic water fight at the edge of the lake. I spotted Maddy and Julie, running hand in hand, squealing as Kurt dumped a pail of water on their heads. On the other end of the beach, DJ was surrounded by a circle of Tadpoles. He had his cast wrapped in a black plastic garbage bag, and each time the little kids splashed him, he'd screech and jump around like an orangutan, scratching at his armpit with his good hand. The more ridiculous he looked, the more the kids splashed and screamed with laughter.

No one was paying any attention to us. I dug my feet in the sand, closed my eyes, and imagined myself starting to swim—my arms shooting sprays of water in a steady one-two rhythm, and my head tilting to the side to gulp air. I visualized myself gliding across the water like someone in the Olympics. But what if there was a current? What if it sucked me under and I couldn't swim back? In my mind, I saw my legs beginning to sink. My arms were still flying one-two, one-two, but my legs were deadweights, dragging my body deeper into the lake. I couldn't touch the bottom with my toes, and no matter how hard I pumped my arms, I couldn't hold myself above the surface. I turned my head to the side and gulped, but there wasn't any air. And then I glimpsed the flash of a tail, wild hair . . . and fangs.

"It's not working," I said. "I can't visualize it."

"Difficult Is Just a Challenge," Mom said. "Break it into Action Steps. Can you imagine putting your toes in?"

I nodded.

"How about your ankles? And your shins?"

"Sure, but that's not swimming."

"If I only set up one consultation today, is that my Pollination Goal for the month?"

"No," I said. "But that's different. You're laying the groundwork."

"Exactly!" Mom pushed a stray strand of hair behind my ear. "Lay some groundwork today, and tomorrow, you'll be that much closer to your goal."

I knew she was trying to be nice, but I pulled the hair back out of place. She didn't get it. She loved swimming. Sticking her head into Thunder Lake was a treat for her. Besides, as far as I could tell, *her* groundwork wasn't bringing us much closer to anything. She'd added a few Potentials to her whiteboard, but her sales numbers hadn't budged, mostly because she wasn't following her own rules. She'd been a Negative Nelly all weekend, and she'd barely prepared for tomorrow's B&B Home Party, which I'd practically had to force her to plan.

"Speaking of goals," I said. "How come Maddy's mom isn't on your Potentials list? She's the one you need to target, don't you think?"

"It's complicated."

"Not really," I said. It wasn't at all complicated. If she didn't sign up enough Worker Bees to get promoted to Queen Bee, that was her own business. But the month-end bonus wasn't about her, it was about the rent. She could try a little harder for Mr. Li. She could certainly try harder for me.

"Is she coming to the Home Party tomorrow?" I asked. "Did you at least invite her?"

Mrs. Nueske's whistle blew, and Mom looked relieved.

"You'd better head to class, sweetie. Good luck!"

Shari the Tadpole Helper handed out white foam kickboards, and we spent the hour practicing float-and-kick techniques. It was surprisingly easy. The kickboard held you out of the water enough so you didn't have to put your face in, and all you had to do was let your legs float up to the surface of the water and kick. The straighter your legs were, the more powerful the kick turned out to be.

Josh and I were paired up for a race, and I gave it everything I had, zooming along at top speed like Namor, the Prince of Atlantis, in an X-Men battle. I could hear DJ yelling, "Go, Anthoni!" from the beach. I grinned. So what if I was only beating a kindergartner? I felt weightless and strong.

"Great work, kids," Shari said as we turned in our kickboards. "Next week, we'll add our breathing exercises. Like this." She held the board out in front of her and stuck her head in the water. As she kicked, she'd turn her head to the side to take a breath of air, then put her face back in. I groaned. It was useless. I'd never be able to do that.

DJ practically ran me over as I stepped onto the beach. He threw my towel at my face. "I nabbed this from your mom. Nice swimming."

"Thanks."

I hugged the towel and tried to stop shivering. DJ picked at a scab on his knee.

"So . . . see you on the flip side."

"Okay," I said, though I didn't have a clue what he was talking about. Julie was right. DJ was an odd duck.

He got halfway up the beach before he tripped over a sandcastle. "I'm good!" he yelled as he brushed himself off and ran toward his aunt's car, holding his cast in the air like a brandished sword.

DJ was easily the klutziest person I'd met. It had taken me and Charlotte ten minutes to get him out from under the booth at The Showboat. Somehow he'd gotten his foot wedged beneath the seat, and since he couldn't put weight on his cast, he'd tried to shimmy his way out and ended up with his head stuck between the table leg and the booth.

"That kid is a walking disaster."

I turned to find Maddy, Kurt, and Julie standing behind me. Julie was carefully toweling off the blistering poison-ivy rashes on her arms.

Kurt pretended to trip and fall. "I'm good," he said in a dopey voice, making Maddy and Julie laugh.

I glared at him.

Maddy wore a black bikini with the Wolverine towel wrapped around her waist, and from the look on her face, it was clear she'd forgotten all about laughing, reading comics, and sharing secrets together.

"You know DJ?" she asked. The tone of her voice told me the correct answer was "No," but I nodded.

"He lives by The Showboat," I said.

"That dude's a nutjob," Kurt said. "Runs in the family. I heard his dad's in a mental ward."

I scowled at Kurt. DJ probably *was* a walking disaster, and he certainly was one of the strangest kids I'd known, but at least he wasn't a jerk.

"So what if he is?" I said. "No one in your family's ever had to go to the hospital before?"

Julie gave a guilty glance in Maddy's direction before she said, "I think it's cool you're friends with DJ. He's kind of gooney, but I guess that's okay. It's probably hard for some people to be normal all the time, and even gooney people need friends, so it's nice you can do that. If you come to Maddy's for fireworks on the Fourth, maybe you could bring DJ."

Kurt groaned. "Come on, Julie. DJ?"

"Don't worry," Maddy said. "I don't invite snoops, thieves, or vandals."

Julie sucked air through her braces and whispered, "Is DJ a vandalizer?"

"I . . ." I didn't know how to start. Of course I deserved it. I couldn't take back snooping in Maddy's closet or almost kidnapping her dolphin, but I felt like if I could make her remember how much fun we'd had together, the real Maddy would come back. The smiling, quiet, fun Maddy. I tried to think of something clever, some inside joke that would remind her that we were destined to be friends.

All I could come up with was, "I shouldn't have snooped in your closet, and I didn't mean to knock over your stuffed dolphins. I'm sorry." I meant it, too.

Maddy's whole body stiffened.

Julie looked like someone had stabbed her in the heart. "You let Anthoni go into your studio?" she asked, but Kurt's cackling drowned her voice out.

"Stuffed *dolphins*?" He doubled over. "Quinn, you've been holding out on us!"

Maddy's eyes went all stony, and Kurt tried to wipe the smile off his face, but a smirk slipped out. "You don't really have a furry dolphin collection, do you?"

"At least I'm not a thief. Or a liar," Maddy said.

Clearly, this wasn't going well. I tried to focus on Maddy's smile. Maybe if I focused on that smile hard enough, it would come back and Evil Maddy would disappear. This wasn't the real her. I knew it couldn't be.

"I wanted to see more of your Lexie drawings," I said. "They're so good."

"You're still doing those drawings?" Julie squeaked, but Maddy didn't look at her. "Of the scary *mermaid*?"

The mermaid. It was my only hope.

"I wasn't lying about the mermaid," I said.

It was risky to say it at Maddy's house, and it was even riskier to say it now. On a public beach. In front of Julie and Kurt. Even though Mom and I had read online about vaudeville and the Boulays' mermaid act, the article *did* say it was so realistic that people believed it was true. What if those people were right? What if Charlotte was serious when she'd said "magic" and "gills" helped her breathe underwater? Even though I knew better, there was still that word hovering in the back of my mind: *Maybe.*

Most importantly, I couldn't stop thinking about how great it felt laughing until my sides hurt in the *Ski Nautique* and smiling my face off in Maddy's room. All warm and fuzzy. Happy. Mom's newsletter quote kept running in my head like a mantra: *Discover Her Secret Dream. Do What It Takes.*

"I can *show* you the mermaid," I said.

This put Kurt over the edge. He held his stomach like it hurt him to laugh so hard. "No wonder DJ likes her," he said. "They're perfect for each other. Nutjobs in looove."

"I'm not . . . I don't even . . ." I sighed. "That's really not cool, Kurt."

"It *sounds* like you guys had a great time," Julie said. She scratched furiously at one of the scabs on her arm. "I'm glad you got to bond so much while I was busy writhing in pain. You know, people can die from poison ivy if they get it bad enough, but I'm glad you didn't worry about me. I wouldn't want to ruin all the fun."

I tried to block it all out—the beach, Julie's poison ivy, Kurt's laugh. I had to focus. Positive Thoughts Attract

Positive Results. *Maddy's smile*, I thought, *Maddy's smile, Maddy's smile*. And then, like a miracle, something in Maddy's eyes shifted. Her stony stare softened, then brightened.

"Okay, show me," she said. And after she said it, she shot me the smile I'd been hoping for. I felt disoriented, like I'd been on one of those anti-gravity rides and my feet couldn't remember what to do on the ground.

Julie stopped itching. She looked hard at Maddy, and then at me. "Is this for real? Don't do it without me, okay? I want to come. Please?"

Kurt was gleeful. "This ought to be good. I'm in."

"Great," I said. My voice sounded like it was coming out of someone else's head. Relief and dread battled it out inside my brain, and depending on which won, I was either going to do backflips right there on the spot or puke my guts out. I took a deep breath. I had to keep it together. I had a mermaid to produce.

24
TRUE OR FALSE

Mom mixed lemonade while I set out sixteen shades of Healthy Honey Glow Eye Shadow on the picnic table in the kitchen. She was still in her swimsuit, even though the guests were coming in less than an hour.

"Why do we have so many eye shadows?" I asked. "There are twelve cases here."

"I had to buy some extra product last month to keep our numbers up."

Mom waved her hand like it was no big deal, but I frowned. How'd she pay for that? With the rent money? The credit card?

"Don't *worry*, we'll sell it," Mom said. She turned up the music, but I still heard her add, "Eventually."

I couldn't stop thinking up ways Mom should have done things differently. She hadn't sent out sample packs in April. In May, she'd skipped the promotional postcards. If you want to succeed, you need to complete all the Action Steps in your plan. That's the way it works. Anything else is giving up. We had less than a week until the end of the month. If we wanted that bonus, this party had to go perfectly. Five Worker Bees—or one at the Premium level—weren't going to recruit themselves.

I almost didn't hear the knock on the door, but Mom cut the music and shot me a panicked look. I knew the ladies from the beach were excited for the party, but who would arrive an hour early? I glared back at her.

"I *told* you there wasn't time for another swim," I said.

Mom grabbed a towel to cover up her swimsuit and shooed me toward the door.

"You entertain them, I'll go change."

I opened the door to find Maddy Quinn on the other side of the screen, her hands resting on the handles of an orange dirt bike. What was she doing here?

"My mom says thanks for the invite, but she's not coming," she said. "It's not really her thing."

"Okay." I tried to act like it was no big deal, but Mrs. Quinn was our only Premium-level Potential. How did she know it wasn't her thing if she'd never even tried it? Now Mom was going to have to get five Worker Bees to sign up today or find a way to prove to Maddy's mom that she was missing out.

Meanwhile, Maddy was still standing in front of The Blue Heron.

"Do you . . . want to come in?"

"No. I've got ski practice."

"Cool."

Maddy stuck her hand in her pocket and pulled out a folded square of paper. A note? Did Maddy Quinn write me a note? She tossed the paper onto the doormat.

"That's for you," she said, then hopped on her bike and rode away.

Mom raced out of the bedroom in a bright-yellow sundress and pulled a batch of honey muffins out of the oven.

"Who's here?" she asked.

"Maddy," I said, shoving the note in my pocket. "Do you need more help? I really want to go outside."

"Yeah, I need you to . . ." Mom saw the look on my face and gave the room a quick survey. "I can take it from here. You go have fun with your friend, sweetie."

I threw on my backpack and sandals and wandered down the path through the woods, unfolding the note as I walked. It was a hand-drawn comic:

GILLS: A MYSTERY
by Maddy H. Quinn

The first panel showed a fish with a dolphin in its mouth. The lettering read: *Dolphin-stealer? Confirmed.*

In the second panel, the fish was reading a comic. *Marvel girl? So she says.*

In the third panel, there were *two* smiling fish, both in diapers with pink bows on their heads. *Best friend? Once upon a time . . .*

The final panel was broken into two sections. In one half, the fish wore a halo and had a giant, gold heart in its chest. Block letters shouted *IS GILLS TRUE?* In the other half, the fish's heart was being devoured by Lexie. *OR FALSE?* Drops of blood dripped down her chin and formed themselves into the words: *To be continued . . .*

I couldn't keep my eyes off the happy baby fish. *Best friend? Once upon a time . . .*

Maddy didn't remember me as some kid she went to kindergarten and had a few laughs with. She remembered me as her *best friend.* True Blue was only one step away. I'd never been this close before. Messing it up was not an option.

I heard a wild crunching of leaves and sticks, like a bear crashing through the forest, and I was on my butt before I knew what hit me.

"Sorry, Gills!" DJ's face flashed red. "I tried to slow down. Pine needles are slippery."

I shoved the note in my pocket and brushed the dirt off my backpack.

"Do you ever watch where you're going?" I asked.

"Mmm . . . not really," DJ said. "Anyway, I was running to find you. So that worked out."

The kitchen of The Black Bear had been fully transformed into a rock museum. I picked up a piece of DJ's Baraboo Quartzite and rubbed it in my hands, hoping the whole Wolverine stronger-under-pressure thing would rub off. The way this summer was going, I could use all the help I could get.

"Here." DJ handed me a heavy wooden jewelry box. "Check it out."

I set down the quartzite. The box was engraved with the words:

100% CERTIFIED AUTHENTICITY
Genuine Precious Stones
from the Underwater City of Atlantis
PROPERTY OF HERACLITUS BARNABUS BOULAY

I opened the box and lifted a purple velvet cover from the inside. Three rocks sat nested in the center. The first was a bumpy, gray rock the shape of a giant egg. The tag next to it read: *Collected from the Great Stone Portal to the Watery World.* The second was similar to a piece of finger-length coral, but it changed from purple to blue to green as it shone and sparkled in the light. *Collected from the Dazzling Outcroppings of the Western Realms*. The third stone was as tiny as a thumbnail— gold, and perfectly round. *An Unprecedented Gift from the Trident of King Triton Himself.*

"Where'd you find this?"

"On the kitchen counter," DJ said.

He held up a note that said *For DJ. Signed, CB*.

"There's something for you."

He handed me a paper bag scrawled with a giant "A." There were two framed photos inside. One was the picture of the Boulay Mermaid I'd tried to smuggle off in my backpack. The other was of Lady Alice and her Dirty Rats.

"Why doesn't she want these anymore?" I asked.

"Who knows?" DJ said. "Why does she have a secret doorway? Why does she talk in weird accents? Why does she dance like two people at once . . ."

"Fair enough."

I examined the face of the miniature Boulay Mermaid. Her smile was wide and cocked to the side. Her crooked tooth jutted out over her bottom lip. That smile was Charlotte Boulay, through and through.

"I still think it could be true," I said. I wasn't being hopeful or trying to *make* it true. I meant it. But I was surprised I'd said it out loud.

"What could?"

I turned the photo toward him and DJ got a big, silly grin on his face.

"You think I'm gullible," I said.

"Yeah," he said, still grinning his freckles off. "It's awesome!"

"Gullible is awesome?"

DJ nodded. "Kind of. People usually think *I'm* the one who's goofy. It's nice to be on the other side."

"Thanks a lot," I said.

DJ patted my shoulder awkwardly with his cast. "I meant it in a good way. Here," he said, clearing a space on the table. "Give me a piece of your notebook paper."

"Why?"

"We'll figure it out like geologists. We'll make a list of attributes and see how they match up."

I wasn't 100-percent sure if he was being serious or making fun, but it was a decent idea. I was surprised I hadn't thought of it myself. I fished my notebook and pencil out of my backpack.

"Okay, Appearance first," he said. "Does she have a tail?"

"Not exactly, but . . ." I glanced at the photo of the Boulay Mermaid.

"Write *undetermined*," DJ said. "For all we know, she could be under some kind of spell where her tail grows back once she's underwater."

I gave him a suspicious look, but he seemed to be taking this seriously, so I wrote down: *Tail—undetermined.*

"Okay now, Characteristics. You said she can swim really far?"

"I saw her go all the way to the edge of the bay without coming up for air," I said.

DJ nodded. "Promising."

I started to write down *Breathes underwater*, but DJ held out his hand.

"We've only determined *Swims far*," he said. "Didn't she say she uses breathing tubes?"

"She also said 'gills.' And 'magic.'"

"True," DJ said. "Plus, a tube would never work. You'd be breathing out oxygen and breathing in carbon dioxide. Unless she has some kind of air compressor or she's talking about a snorkel. Maybe scuba gear . . ."

"She didn't have *any* of that when she jumped in."

"Right." DJ thought about it. For all his gooey exterior, he was more logical and organized than you'd think.

"*Method uncertain,*" he concluded.

In the end, our list looked like this:

> Tail—undetermined
> Swims far
> Breathes underwater—method uncertain
> Prone to strange behavior

Prone to odd jokes

Boulay photo—looks real, could be fake

Rocks from Atlantis—look fake, could be real

"It's not a lot to go on," I said. "I don't think she's going to be convinced."

"Who?"

"Maddy."

"Quinn? What do you care what she thinks?"

"She's nicer than she seems," I said. "I think."

"If you say so. I wouldn't tell her about the mermaid, though."

I pretended to study the box of Genuine Precious Stones. "Why not?"

"Maddy likes to be queen. If you give her a chance to lord something over you, she will. It would be a disaster."

"You don't know her," I said, feeling annoyed. "You've only lived here a year."

"So? You've been here two weeks," DJ said. "You can believe whatever you want to believe, but it doesn't make it true."

I grabbed my notebook and shoved it in my backpack. What did he know? He was happy playing with kindergartners. Or rocks. He wouldn't understand what it meant to have a True Blue Friend—someone who liked the same things you liked and had your back no matter what happened or how far away you were. Someone who wanted to invite you for sleepovers and made you feel like you *belonged.* I stuffed Lady Alice and her Dirty Rats in my pack behind the notebook.

"Hey," DJ said. "I didn't mean . . ."

He picked up the Boulay Mermaid photo at the exact moment that I reached for it, and like a slow-motion scene in a movie, we watched the frame tumble from our fingers to the table to the bench to the kitchen floor. The photo wasn't in a heavy-duty frame like Alice and the rest of the gang on The Showboat's walls. It was ornate and delicate and it shattered with a high-pitched *clang.*

We stared at the shards.

"I'm sorry, Gills," DJ said in a tortured voice. "I'm such a . . ."

I shushed him. "What do you think that is?"

The man, the woman, and the Boulay Mermaid smiled at us beneath the broken bits of glass. Behind the photo, where the frame had split, the corner of a pink envelope peeked out.

The envelope wasn't sealed, and it didn't hold a love letter or a note written in secret code. It was filled with several carefully folded newspaper clippings. Obituaries, to be exact. The top one, from the *Milwaukee Sentinel,* was dated July 6, 1942, and featured a photo of the smiling lady in the Boulay Mermaid picture.

SELINA BOULAY—VAUDEVILLE
HOLD-OUT—DIES, AGE 34

EAGLE WATERS, WI—Selina Boulay, daughter of famed
actress Alice VanEllsburgh and daughter-in-law of vaudeville
veteran Barnabus Boulay, died yesterday in a tragic accident
at The Showboat Resort in Eagle Waters, Wisconsin. Born into
vaudeville, Mrs. Boulay was best known for her family novelty
act, "The Famous Boulays Present: The Darling Boulay Mermaid." Selina Boulay is survived by her husband, Frank Boulay,
age 36, and her daughter, Charlotte, age 12.

A tragic accident? My eyes focused on the last phrase.
"Survived by . . . her daughter, Charlotte, age 12." Mom
was thirty-four. And I was almost twelve. Even though
I'd been mad at her lately, I couldn't imagine life without her. Who would laugh at my robot dances and put
her arm around me when I had a bad day? Who would
cheer me up with Green Goddess smoothies and sing
along with the radio until we went hoarse? If something
happened to Mom, I'd be more than lost. I'd be completely alone.

"Poor Charlotte," I said.

DJ tucked the clippings back in the envelope. His
face wasn't red, it was white. Gray, almost. Deliberately,
he stood up and left the cabin, letting the screen door
slap shut behind him.

25

GRAVITY

I found DJ on the wooden bleachers that led down to the dock. He sat perfectly still, staring out at Thunder Lake.

"You okay?" I asked.

"Shhh." DJ held up his cast.

I stopped moving and scanned the area, trying to see what he was looking at.

"What?" I whispered. "What is it?"

DJ pointed to a shallow, weedy area to the left of the dock.

"Blue heron."

The gray-blue feathers blended so well with the water and the weeds that I almost missed it. A bird stood in the shallows, still as a statue, balancing on its spindly, twig-like legs.

Quietly, I sat down next to DJ. The heron seemed to be listening or watching for something. Its long neck stretched forward, and a breeze lifted a few of its feathers. It looked ancient and exotic, like a miniature velociraptor who got left behind when the dinosaurs went extinct. Suddenly, the heron stabbed the water with its beak and pulled out a gigantic frog.

"Nasty!" DJ hissed.

The frog wriggled and thrashed and nearly escaped, but the heron tilted its head, tightening and adjusting the frog's position in its beak. When the frog was in the right spot, the heron threw back its head and gulped. The bird gulped and gulped, forcing the frog down its skinny throat.

We watched the bulge slide slowly down the bird's neck, and when it got about halfway, DJ grabbed my arm. The heron had stopped moving. But it wasn't the intense stillness we'd seen when it was hunting the frog. The heron swayed a little, and its legs began to bend. The bird looked woozy.

DJ's grip tightened on my arm, and we gasped as the heron jerked back to life, gulping again until the bulge disappeared. Then, the bird stretched its wings, tilted its head, and began to walk, slowly and carefully, away from the dock.

DJ turned to look at me. His eyes were huge. "I thought he was going to keel over," he said, still whispering.

"Hey, DJ," I whispered back.

"Yeah?"

"You're crushing my arm."

DJ looked down, clearly surprised to find that his good hand had my wrist in a death grip. Even his ears turned fuchsia.

"Sorry," he said, stretching out his fingers. "That was insane."

We sat in silence. I hadn't believed Charlotte's impression of the choking heron for one minute. I thought it was a joke, but now I wondered how many of the things she'd told me had been true. I thought about how happy she looked in the photo with her mom and dad, everyone smiling like movie stars. Not like the way her eyebrows had pinched together when she'd told us about her dad going to jail, or when she'd thrown her head back and yelled, "The weight of the past!" No wonder it felt so heavy. If anything happened to Mom, I'd probably be flattened under the weight of it.

DJ looked a little flattened now, too. I remembered what Kurt had said at the beach, about DJ's dad being in the hospital.

"How come you live with your aunt?" I asked.

DJ kept his voice low. The heron was still making its way along the shore, head bobbing forward with each step. "My dad has a chemical thing in his brain that makes him depressed," he said. "It's not a huge deal. Most of the time he's fine, but right now he needs help getting back on his feet. He'll be home soon."

"And your mom?"

DJ picked up a pinecone and started to pick off each scaly piece, tossing them one by one into the lake.

"She died a while ago. My dad really misses her. It's hard for him."

"Is it hard for you?"

"Not usually. Sometimes it just hits you." DJ shot me a sideways glance. "She was cool. Guess what her job was?"

"What?"

"Geologist." He grinned. "She studied rocks and got paid for it. How rad is that?"

We watched each pinecone scale hit the water without a sound, then spin and drift. A few clumped together, colliding like bumper cars, and others floated off into the distance all alone. When the entire pinecone was scattered onto Thunder Lake, DJ brushed his hand on his pants.

"How come you don't like to put your face in the water, Gills?" he asked.

"I don't know," I said, letting him change the subject. "I keep thinking I'll be brave enough to do it, but the water is so dark. How do you know what's in there?

How do you know how deep it is? Every time I try to put my head in, I get this panicky feeling that I can't get rid of."

DJ nodded like he knew exactly what I was talking about.

"It's gravity that gets me," he said, holding up his cast.

I laughed.

"I'm serious," he said. "I love heights. When you climb a tree, it's like all your problems are underneath your feet." He pointed to the heron, who had stopped taking slow steps away and paused, with its wings slightly spread. "The problem is, if I let myself look down, I know gravity will pull me right back."

With a splash and flutter, the heron spread its wings and lifted off, tucking its feet underneath its body and soaring across the bay.

DJ stood up just as suddenly. "I don't stop climbing trees, though," he said. "Wait here!"

He took off running up the stairs.

While I waited, I rummaged through my backpack. I took out Josh's deflated floaties and blew one up out of boredom. SpongeBob SquarePants got bigger and wider. I slid it over my right arm, but it only went as far as my elbow. I let out some air and tugged the floatie all the way up to my armpit. It fit nice and snug.

I blew up the second floatie and put it on my left

arm. I made fists in the air, holding my arms out like the muscle woman at a circus.

"Nice biceps," DJ said, barreling back down the stairs.

I did a couple strong-arm poses to make him laugh.

"Here, try these." DJ handed me a pair of blue swim goggles.

"No thanks."

"Try them."

"My mom said I can't swim without an adult around."

"We're not going to." DJ pulled a second pair of goggles over his own head.

"You look like a bug-eyed mutant," I said.

DJ did an alien dance to play up the effect. He alien-danced all the way down to the edge of the dock and lay down on his belly. "Come on," he said.

I lay down next to him and pulled the blue goggles on.

"Nice. Look. Fellow. Mutant," he said in a robotic voice.

"Mutants don't talk like robots," I said. "Unless they're actual robots."

DJ leaned his shoulders over the dock. The water shimmered inches below his nose and he splashed his head down into the lake. When he came up again, he shook the water out of his hair like a dog.

"No way," I said. "I'm not doing that."

"Fine," he said. "But think about it. This way, you can

get a good look while the rest of your body is safe on land." He shrugged his shoulders at me. "It's drown-proof research. At least you'll know what's down there."

I *was* curious.

"Besides, you're already wearing a snazzy pair of floaties. How safe can you get?"

"I don't know . . ."

"Plug your nose," he said. "It'll help."

I plugged my nose with one hand, gripped the dock with the other, and stared into Thunder Lake. *Happy thoughts, happy thoughts. Maddy being nice. DJ climbing a tree.* I plunged my face in. A floaty sensation filled my ears, and I immediately sat up, gasping for air.

"Are you okay?" DJ asked.

I nodded.

"See anything?"

I shook my head. "I forgot to open my eyes." I felt the dock, solid underneath me, and added, "But it wasn't that bad."

I took a deep breath and tried it again. This time, I stayed down a little longer and opened my eyes. I didn't see a thing. Only murky, brown water. The third time, my eyes adjusted more. I could see green weeds floating on the bottom of the lake and DJ's hand pointing to a bunch of tiny fish swimming all in the same direction.

"Minnows," he said when we popped up.

To tell the truth, there wasn't much to see. More

minnows. More weeds. Sand. Rocks. It wasn't nearly as creepy as I'd thought it would be. Each time I put my head in, I felt lighter, happier, more powerful. I was taming Thunder Lake. Until a black fish the size of my foot swam into view. I was so startled, I gulped in water, and lifted my head, coughing.

"It's only a sucker," DJ said.

"Will it bite?"

He laughed. "Every fish in this lake thinks you're a gigantic monster that wants to eat it. They're not going to bite you. Watch."

We put our heads back down, and DJ reached his arm into the water, waving it in the direction of the sucker. The fish darted away from the dock, and swam toward a large pile of rocks off in the distance. It was hard to see clearly in the murky water, but there was something un-natural about the pile. The rocks looked familiar—gray, bumpy, and egg-shaped—and they were piled perfectly into a rounded, waist-high mound. Something thin and flexible, like a braid or a rope, swayed in the water nearby. I followed it with my eyes. The rope connected to a long, skinny pipe shooting out the side of the rock mound. The rope and the pipe extended together toward the middle of the lake until the water became so deep and dark I couldn't see them anymore. I jerked my head out of the lake and sat up.

"Drown-proof research!" DJ said, ripping his goggles

off and shaking them at me. His eyes were rimmed with red raccoon circles. "I'm a genius!"

"So you saw that?"

"How fast he swam? Yeah, I told you. You're a monster."

"No, the . . . hold on." The sun went behind a cloud and a cold breeze blew across Thunder Lake. I shivered as I put my head down one more time. Without the sun shining, the water was even murkier. No matter how hard I squinted, I couldn't see anything but ropy weeds and shadows.

"What'd you see?" DJ asked when I came up for air.

Part of me wanted to say "Nothing." It wasn't exactly a lie. With the sun behind the clouds, there was nothing to see. Which meant it could all still be true. *Tail— undetermined. Swims far. Breathes underwater—method uncertain.*

Maybe.

But even though it meant giving up magic and *maybe* and possibly even Maddy Quinn, I couldn't fake it. I knew what I saw.

"Breathing tubes," I said.

26

GILLIS GIRLS DON'T BELIEVE IN MAYBE

I banged open the screen door and dropped my back-pack on the floor. I felt like a fool. It was bad enough that I'd *believed* in the Boulay Mermaid, but what was I going to do on Monday? Show up at swim lessons and say, *Hey, guys, that whole mermaid thing? Just joking! Hilarious, right?* Maddy Quinn would never forgive me. I might as well give up now. It would be easier to quit swim lessons and hide in the cabin until Mom finished saving the money we needed to leave.

"Anthoni Marie Gillis! What was the one rule I gave you this summer?"

My hair, still dripping wet from the lake, had soaked the shoulders of my T-shirt. Mom took one look at me and went ballistic.

"Mom, I didn't . . ."

"You didn't go in the water? What'd you do, then, take a shower?" She was seething. "One rule, Anthoni. I only gave you one rule!"

I was all off-kilter. Mom hardly ever got mad, and when she did, it was never at me. I tried to explain quickly. "I didn't go in. Just my head. With goggles. And floaties. It was safe."

I sat down at the picnic table. It was covered with used eye shadows, partially filled cups of lemonade, and paperwork from Mom's B&B party.

"Look at me when I'm talking to you," Mom said. "Your head? Water? Go on."

I explained about the goggles again, but I couldn't help stealing glances at Mom's Home Party sales sheet. One $10.50 Bee-You-tiful Lipstick sale and one $15 Zit Stinger sale. A grand total of $25.50—which probably wouldn't even cover the cost of all the free samples the ladies took home. The Worker Bee sign-up section was completely blank.

"Anthoni, are you even listening to me?"

"Are you listening to *me*? I put my head in! I thought you'd be glad."

Mom looked conflicted, like she suddenly didn't know whether to yell at me or not.

"Anthoni, I'm glad you overcame your fear and put your head in the water. I really am." She bit her lip. "But

I need to be able to trust you to do the right thing when I'm not around."

The words "not around" got my attention. I knew Mom meant it like, "when I'm not around because I'm at the grocery store," but the news about DJ's mom—and Charlotte Boulay's for that matter—was fresh in my mind.

"I'm sorry," I said.

Mom sat next to me on the bench. "You could get hurt. I couldn't take that. Especially not today." She closed her eyes and rubbed her forehead. Three whole tears slipped down her cheeks.

That stunned me. Mom never cried. Not with actual tears. Ever.

"I mean it," I said. "I'm really sorry."

Another tear.

"I'm okay. I didn't get hurt. Look. I promise." I did a goofy arm dance to show her I was in 100-percent working order.

Mom wiped at her eyes. "It's not really that," she said.

I glanced at the Home Party sales sheet again.

"There are still three days left until the end of the month," I said. "If you work hard, you could get Mrs. Quinn, and that would be enough to get the bonus."

Mom put her hand on my knee. "It's not going to happen, honey."

"Mom! Negative Thoughts . . ."

"I had a call from one of the Hive Directors," she said. "If I don't pull my team together, I'm going to be demoted to Worker Bee."

Demoted. I heard the word, but I couldn't let it sink in. I let it float above my head, hovering at a safe distance so I wouldn't have to think about what it meant if we'd wasted the last five years.

Mom wiped another tear and tried to smile. "I need to do my job better. I should have stayed focused and instead I dragged us up here. I thought it would buy us time, but you've been miserable, and I . . ."

She hiccupped and sniffed, really losing it now.

"I'm not miserable," I said. "I like it here."

I was surprised to realize it was true. I *did* like it. I liked The Showboat Resort. It was creepy and deserted, but it was interesting and unpredictable. Even without magic or mermaids, Mom had been right—there was a *feeling* about the place. In fact, if I really thought about it, this was the first place we'd been that felt something like home.

"You don't have to say that." She sniffed. "Anyway, we'll leave on Thursday, okay?"

I sat up straight. "Thursday? That's two days from now."

"I know. I was going to suggest tomorrow, but I can't handle another speed-packing session."

"We'll lose the deposit. We haven't even been here three weeks."

"I talked to Charlotte today. She said she'd prorate us. As a favor to you. You must have made a good impression when you brought her that sample pack."

This was not how things were supposed to go. The Mom I knew wouldn't throw in the towel on a month-end bonus when there were still three days left. She would get a plan together, pull a couple all-nighters, and Do What It Takes to get the job done.

"We can't go back to Mr. Li," I said. "He could . . ." What could he do? Report us? Put Mom in jail for not paying the rent? I was starting to feel like I couldn't breathe, like I was sucking in water I couldn't spit out.

"We'll go to Chicago," Mom said. "Kimmy said we can stay with her. My best Worker Bees are there. It's where I'll have the best chance to get our team back on track."

I didn't want to cry, but my eyes filled up anyway. Minutes ago, I'd been fantasizing about quitting swim lessons and hiding in the cabin until we could leave The Showboat. But the thought of *actually* leaving made me dig in my heels. I wanted to stay. Badly.

"You're the one who wanted to come here," I said. I could feel the tears slipping out of the corners of my eyes, one for every promise she'd made that hadn't come true. "You said it was magical. All we had to do was think positive. Stick to the plan."

"Well, maybe not every plan is worth sticking to!" Mom snapped. She stood up and walked to the window. "Maybe sometimes you have to know when to give up on a plan."

Give up?

"What happened to 'Gillis Girls Don't Believe in Maybe'? You said you were going to *fix* everything!"

"Anthoni, I have to take care of my team."

For a moment, I felt like I was back underwater with DJ's goggles tight around my hair, minnows and weeds drifting in and out of sight. Blood rushed to my head, thumping in my ears as I held my breath. Did she even hear herself? Her *team*?

"What about taking care of *me*?" I shouted, hot tears sliding down my cheeks. "You might not have noticed, but I don't have any friends. Not one. I don't even have Gramps anymore because *you* put him in a home. What if something happened to you? I'd have nobody. *Not. One. Person!* Do you ever think about *that*?"

The words and the tears kept pouring out. It was like a floodgate had opened, and I couldn't stop them if I tried. I felt my hand crumple her Home Party sales sheet and throw it at her.

"You stole from Mr. Li!" I yelled. "You can call it a detour or buying time, but really, you're just a thief!"

Mom winced like I'd slapped her in the face, and I looked away so I wouldn't have to see how badly I'd hurt her feelings. But yelling never worked on Mom. It only made her more stubborn. She smoothed her hair and pulled herself together. Her tears were gone.

"Anthoni, it is what it is," she said calmly. "Chicago is the new plan. Now, change your state and start packing."

I threw my backpack over my shoulders. My whole life, she'd been telling me all you needed to succeed was a plan and the guts to stick to it, no matter how tough things got. And now, apparently, she didn't believe it, or she didn't have the guts. Well, I did. I wasn't going to be like her. I wasn't going to get this far and give up.

I walked out of The Blue Heron and slammed the screen door behind me. Mermaid or no mermaid, I had a plan and I was sticking to it.

27
DEATH OF VAUDEVILLE

I went to The Black Bear first, hoping to catch DJ sorting his rocks, but no one was there. The wooden bear looked devastated.

"It's all right, buddy," I said, and patted him on the head. We stood together for a while, watching a squirrel make loud tsk-ing noises at us from a high branch. I tried to remember what Chicago was like. I was seven when we lived there last, and all I could recall about our apartment was that the wallpaper in the bathroom had lollipops on it. I wondered what our new bathroom would look like and if any kids my age would live in our apartment building. The thought of making a new Potentials list made me tired.

The squirrel started throwing acorns at my head, so

I left the cub to fend for himself and continued down the path toward the hotel.

I heard the music blasting even before I got out of the woods.

The front office was empty, but somewhere behind the revolving bookcase a woman belted out, "I'm always chasing ra-a-a-ain-bows."

"Hello?" I could hardly hear myself over the song.

I walked halfway across the room before I noticed that all the photos DJ and I had cleaned and boxed up were back on the walls. The frog-man, the tap dancers, the hula girls—every frame had been rehung exactly as it had been before.

The singing stopped and a man started talking. I pushed at the bookcase and stepped through the revolving door into the swanky Showboat Lounge. Charlotte Boulay sat curled up in the center booth, transfixed by a black-and-white movie playing at top volume on a screen above the stage.

"Hello?" I shouted again over the din. Charlotte put a finger to her lips, then beckoned me over without taking her eyes off the screen. Her feet were tucked underneath a long silk bathrobe and her orange hair was hidden under a knot of silk scarves.

"This is my favorite part," she said in a loud whisper as I slid into the other side of her half-moon booth. On the screen, an old man sat at a piano next to a teenage girl with perfect curls. Two men and a blond woman stood next to them, arguing.

"That's Judy Garland," Charlotte said, her eyes still glued to the screen. "She's been in a vaudeville act with her father for years, but now she's trying out for a solo part in a big show called the 'Ziegfeld Follies.'"

The man on the screen clearly didn't like her audition. "Doncha know they quit beating a song to death ten years ago?" he said.

"Now, watch," Charlotte whispered. "She's going to sing it again—her own way, not her father's."

The girl started to sing the song again, only this time she sang it slowly. Instead of a peppy, loud song about someone running after rainbows, it turned out to be a sad song about chasing dreams that never come true. It was beautiful.

When the song was over, Charlotte lifted up a remote and paused the movie. "See?" she said, dreamy-eyed. "Isn't that a great scene?"

"Yeah," I said.

Charlotte leaned closer, examining me. "Rough day?" she asked. "You're looking a little damp."

I felt damp. My throat hurt and my eyes felt swollen and hot.

"I put my head in the lake," I said. "For the first time. I was too scared to do it before. Actually . . . terrified." It felt good to admit it.

"Nicely done," Charlotte said, nodding her approval.

"Thanks," I said.

"I suppose you're here about the gifts?"

I'd almost forgotten about the photos and the stones from Atlantis. "Don't you want them anymore?" I asked.

"You're a good audience, kid. They should belong to someone who can appreciate them. Think of it as a thank-you present."

"For what?" As far as I knew, DJ and I hadn't done anything but break into The Black Bear, spill tea on her floor, and upset her by bringing up the weight of the past.

"For helping me get things in order."

"But you put all the pictures back up."

"True," she said. "I got lonely. It's hard to get rid of the past when it's all you have."

"You have *now*, don't you?"

She raised one eyebrow. "Technically."

I looked at the empty booths in the Showboat Lounge and tried to imagine what the place was like when Charlotte was a kid. I pictured it filled with people dancing and drinking cocktails while Selina Boulay sang on-stage. I bet back then, Charlotte never imagined she'd be sitting here, years later, all alone.

"Did you and your mom ever fight?" I asked.

"What do you mean . . . like fisticuffs? Who do you think I am?"

"No, I mean like a big fight. Where you said horrible things and you couldn't take them back?"

My voice trembled, and Charlotte let out a heavy sigh. She was quiet so long that I started to wonder if she'd forgotten I was there. Finally, she slapped her palm on the table, scaring me half to death.

"You know, kid—want to hear a deep, dark secret?"

I leaned forward across the table. It was impossible, but still, deep down, I felt she was going to admit everything. I wondered if she'd show me her tail, and whether it would be slimy, or glittery, or rough like snakeskin.

"Okay," I said.

Charlotte's eyes drifted downward. Even in the dim glow of the movie screen, I could see the veins on her eyelids.

"When I was your age, I quit the show. I told my mother I hated vaudeville, but I didn't. I loved it."

"Oh." I leaned back against the booth, disappointed.

"That's not the secret."

I inched forward again and waited. Her hand was shaking. She brought it to her mouth and pressed her fingers to her lips. I knew it was possible she was acting. That at any minute, she could erupt with a loud laugh or a "Gotcha!" But she didn't.

"I quit because I thought my mother loved the show more than she loved me," Charlotte said. "Can you imagine feeling like that?"

I could, actually.

"I threw her hairpin in the lake."

I nodded. The pin. The one with the mermaid in the star. Exactly like the one in Maddy's closet. That wasn't so bad. Hardly a deep, dark confession.

"We could find it," I offered. "What if it washed up? What if someone has it and you could get it back?" A very specific someone, in fact.

Charlotte shook her head. "That's sweet, kid," she said. "I'd like to have it back, but it's only a *thing*, see? I lost a lot more than a hairpin that day."

I didn't ask because I knew. She was talking about Selina Boulay.

"They said my mother died because she went off course during rehearsal," Charlotte said. "But I know why. She dove in trying to find that pin. It was my fault. And I never had a chance to say I was sorry."

Charlotte's eyes got watery, but she didn't cry. She just sat there, looking impossibly sad. I was starting to feel teary again, sorry I ran out on Mom. Sorry for yelling at her.

"You must miss her," I said.

Charlotte's eyes swam. I thought if Charlotte cried, my own waterworks might start up, too, so I kept talking.

"Was she good?" I asked. "In the show?"

Charlotte sniffed and lifted her eyes to the ceiling. "She was a star," she said. "An absolute star. There was nothing like it, you know. The energy, the laughs, the applause. Before a show, my mother used to say, 'Chin up, Charlie—let's transport 'em!'"

"Your mom called you Charlie?"

"Atch'r service."

"I wish I could have seen it. Vaudeville."

"Kid, we showed people things they'd never seen, not even in their dreams."

Charlotte's hand had stopped shaking, and the color was slowly returning to her face. A pinprick of an idea flitted into my head.

"What if you could get that feeling again?" I asked.

She chuckled. "That and the vim and vigor of my youth? In exchange for what? Wishes are dangerous things, kid."

Thoughts whirled around in my mind, forming themselves into a plan. A plan with incredible Potential.

"I think I can get your hairpin back," I said. "I know it's only a thing, but wouldn't it be nice to have it again? To remember her by?" I slapped my hand on the table like Charlotte had done. "I need you to do your act."

Her smile disappeared. "My act? Which one? I've got a . . ."

"I know, a million of 'em. I'm talking about the Boulay Mermaid."

We looked at each other across the booth.

Charlotte shook her head and let her feet drop from the cushion to the floor. "It can't be done. Everything's been dismantled."

"But the breathing tubes are still there. And you can swim out into the middle of the lake without coming up for air. Can't you?"

Charlotte narrowed her eyes. "And how, exactly, does the Boulay Mermaid help you?"

"There's this girl. Maddy," I said. "I told her I'd show her a mermaid, and if I do, I think she'll be my True Blue Friend." It sounded dumber than I expected, and I felt my face get DJ-red.

"So the True Blue Friend search continues—despite my fair warning." Charlotte's mouth twitched at the corners. Not like she was laughing at me. Like she knew where I was coming from. Like she understood. "Very well," she said. "Go on."

"I'm always moving from place to place," I said. "And as soon as I'm gone, it's like I never existed."

Charlotte didn't say anything, so I kept going.

"I like it here, and even if the Maddy thing doesn't work, I'd at least like to go out with a bang. So no one can forget me."

"Go out with a bang. That's good. I'd like that, too."

Charlotte closed her eyes, and when she opened them she said, "Okay, now try it again."

"What?"

"The pitch. Try it again. Like you mean it." She winked at me.

I grinned, slid out of the booth, and stood in the light of the movie that was still paused behind me.

"This," I said, "is the single most important decision you could *ever* make. It's a once-in-a-lifetime opportunity to put on the most fabulous, awesome, jaw-dropping show known to mankind!" I threw my arms wildly in the air, stalling for time while my brain grasped for words. "Don't you want to bring some *magic* into the world?"

Then I had a moment of true inspiration.

"Chin up, Charlie!" I shouted. "Let's transport 'em!"

Charlotte Boulay smacked her hands together. "It takes some real work to put on a show like that," she said. "I'm going to need a Master of Ceremonies and a lighting director. Can you make that happen?"

"Absolutely."

"You'll show up to rehearsals?"

"Yes!"

"And do what you're told? No back talk?"

That sounded less appealing, but I agreed.

"What the heck? I'm in." She held out her hand. "One last hurrah. My final curtain call. We'll knock their socks off!"

I reached out my hand and felt Charlotte Boulay's

soft, bony fingers curl around mine. She pumped my arm up and down.

"Welcome to showbiz, kid."

I felt great for about thirty seconds, until I thought about Mom and *her* new plan. Off with the Old and on with the New.

"There's one more thing," I said. "I need your help . . . with a pitch."

28

SEVEN SPECTACULAR DAYS THAT WILL CHANGE THE COURSE OF YOUR LIFE

On my way back to The Blue Heron, I heard Mom calling my name. She was down on the dock, scanning the shore, her hands fluttering nervously at her side. I wasn't sure what to do. I felt horrible for the things I'd said. *Thief.* Was she still mad? I sat down on the top stair.

"I'm here, Mom."

She didn't say a word. Just came to my side and threw her arms around me.

"I've been looking everywhere for you. I was worried," she said when she loosened her hold. She looked awful. Sad and swollen-eyed.

I pulled a twig out of her hair.

"I'm sorry." I couldn't think of how else to say it.

"Me, too."

In the bay, a family of ducks paddled close to the shore, dipping their bills into the murky water. One duckling straggled behind, while the others kept to a tight, fuzzy group.

"You were right, you know," Mom said. "I've made a lot of choices that made things harder on you than they should be. I didn't pay attention to how lonely you were feeling. And I put a lot on your plate. With Beauty & the Bee. And Gramps."

The duckling poked his head into the water and came up with a bill full of weeds.

"It's not fair to you," she said. "I shouldn't be your only person in the world."

"I know. But I'm glad I have you."

Mom put her arm around me.

"Forget 'Gillis Girls Always Stick to the Plan,'" she said. "As long as we stick *together*, we'll pull through."

I nodded. "Gillis Girls always do."

She pulled me close again and I melted into her warm, honey-scented hug. Home.

After dinner, I handed a packet of pages to Mom. The title page read: *A Proposal for Staying Seven More Days, by Anthoni Gillis.* Charlotte had argued for *Seven Spectacular Days That Will Change the Course of Your Life,* but I thought we'd have better luck with a more straight-forward approach. We'd worked all afternoon on the pro-posal. I created flowcharts, checklists, and Action Steps while Charlotte added adjectives and what she called "fuzzy numbers."

"Everybody loves statistics," she'd said. "They're inherently trustworthy."

I did the dishes while Mom flipped through the doc-uments. I wanted to let her concentrate, but it was hard not to watch for her reaction. At some points she smiled, but at others, she rubbed her forehead and groaned. Once, she laughed out loud.

"What's funny?" I asked. I didn't remember putting in any jokes.

"Nothing," she said. "I just didn't know that eighty-nine percent of people who watch fireworks on July Fourth report excellent physical health." She ran her finger down the page. "Or that one in four people who move right before a national holiday suffer from severe acne and, in rare instances, head lice."

I blushed. Some of Charlotte's fuzzy numbers were fuzzier than others. "Those numbers are estimates," I said.

"I see," Mom said, and went back to reading. When she finished, she set the proposal on the table, and patted the seat next to her. I sat down.

"Well?" I asked.

"That was a lot of work," Mom said.

I nodded.

"This is really important to you."

I nodded again.

"I have to admit, aside from some very bizarre statistics, you make some good points," she said. "You could use more swimming lessons. One week is not going to make or break my career. And realistically, I'm not going to be able to do a lot of networking over the holiday when everyone else in the world is on vacation."

"Exactly," I said. "Did you see my cost-benefit analysis? If we leave now, we lose more than we gain if we stay."

"I saw it," Mom said. "It actually made sense." She flipped through the packet again. "Unlike this sentence: *Some countries consider it a federal crime to cut a vacation shorter than originally planned.* What countries?"

"I'll . . . have to check my sources."

"Here's the deal," she said. "We'll stay to watch the fireworks. I'll use the extra days to set up some meetings and checklists for Chicago. But after the Fourth, we're leaving, and I can promise you, no proposal will change my mind."

I jumped out of my seat and threw my arms around her.

"Okay, okay, don't strangle me," Mom said, but she locked me in a bear hug and whispered, "I wanted to see the fireworks, too."

29

CHOPPING WOOD

The next morning, I found a note on the door of The Black Bear.

FIRST REHEARSAL: 2:00 P.M. ON THE DOCK.

DJ showed up five minutes late, and Charlotte read him the riot act, lecturing him about punctuality and the laziness of "kids these days."

"I came, didn't I?" DJ protested. "I don't even know what I'm here for!"

"Greatness!" Charlotte bellowed. "You've heeded the call to greatness! Seize the cup! Fame waits for no man!"

DJ shot me a wary look. Even I wasn't sure what I'd gotten us into.

Charlotte rummaged around in a small trunk on the dock and extracted a hat, a cape, and some lighting equipment.

"What are we doing?" DJ whispered to me while she rifled through the trunk.

I grinned. "The Boulay Mermaid show."

DJ's eyes widened. "Really? How come?"

I hesitated. I could tell him the truth—that it was all an elaborate plan to get a hairpin for Charlotte and help me become the person who made Maddy Quinn's dreams come true. Charlotte had understood. But I wasn't sure about DJ. He didn't like Maddy. He wasn't going to be all gung ho about a plan to get her to like *me*.

"I don't know," I said. "For fun?"

DJ shrugged. "Okay. I'm in."

Two hours later, Charlotte was still barking at us.

"Bing! Boom! Bam! Chop-chop! What is this, amateur night?"

Charlotte slapped her hands together as DJ and I scrambled to our "marks." DJ stood at the spotlight we'd assembled in the bushes, and I flipped my cape and walked down the stairs to the dock.

"Follow her, DJ! Follow her!" Charlotte yelled, even though he seemed to be doing a perfectly good job keeping the spotlight aimed right at me as I moved. Not that we could tell for sure. It was broad daylight, and it was impossible to know whether the light was on me or not. Charlotte said it didn't matter. It was a dry run. We had to get the motions down.

"Ladies and gentlemen," I said, throwing my arms wide and taking the deep bow Charlotte had already made me re-do seven times. "You are about to see something so spectacular, so amazing, that you won't believe your eyes."

"You call that delivery?"

I made my voice even louder. "So specTACular, so aMAZing . . ."

"Yes, YES!" She jumped up and down.

"The Boulay Mermaid is a rare creature," I continued, "born in the clear waters of the South Seas. At a young age, her parents were brutally murdered by a sea serpent, and she was left an orphan. It's sad enough to make a whale blubber."

"Pause for the laughs," Charlotte coached.

"But it's not funny," I said.

"Whale? Blubber? It's gold! Now hit 'em with the sob story."

"Imagine," I said, "being left as a child to fend for yourself. How lonely. How cold. How terrifying."

Charlotte hit herself on the forehead. "How many times do I have to say it? Make eye contact. Sell it! How LONELY, how TERRIFYING." She sobbed. "Tear their hearts out! I'm telling you, it would be much easier if you sang."

This was where my musical number was supposed to come in, but I'd put my foot down. There was no way I was going to dance and sing. I didn't care if it ruined the effect.

"How LONELY! How COLD! How TERRIFYING!" I belted.

"Better. Now take it from the top."

DJ's job was much easier than mine. First, he was in charge of watching the emergency line—a rope that Charlotte would pull if anything went wrong.

"A precaution," she said. "Government regulation. Hardly necessary."

Other than that, all he had to do was follow me with the spotlight. When I got to the part about how the mermaid had been rescued by the Boulays and brought to Thunder Lake, he was supposed to swing the light toward the dock where Charlotte would be sitting. Once she dove into the lake, there were numbers on the spotlight that marked the right angle for each trick. Number one was for her first trick, number two for the second, and so on. It seemed easy enough, but she drilled him on it as hard as she drilled me on my lines.

"One! Four! Three!" she shouted, mixing up the order of the tricks to see if he was paying attention. Rehearsal, she said, was chopping wood. You had to do it again, and again, and again, and again in order to see results.

But she didn't rehearse her own tricks.

"I'm the headliner," she said. "I've been chopping wood since before your grandparents were born. My job isn't to rehearse. It's to go out with a bang. Right, kid?"

We rehearsed all weekend, and on Sunday, Charlotte gave us the game plan. The show would go live on July Fourth.

"It's more dramatic when it happens right after the fireworks. There's something about sparkling lights exploding in the air that preps people to believe in magic. Can you make that happen?"

DJ and I both nodded. I hoped so.

"Fine. Meet me on this dock, in costume, as soon as the brouhaha's all over. Swear you won't be late?"

We linked our pinkies and swore, and even though I knew the Fourth of July would bring fireworks and secret dreams and a True Blue Friend, I couldn't forget it also meant leaving the next day. No more rehearsals, no more zany Charlotte Boulay. Maybe Mom was right and there *was* something magical about The Showboat Resort. Clearly, I was under some kind of spell. How else could you explain how badly I wanted to stay?

After our final rehearsal, DJ stood outside The Black Bear while I shoved my costume in my backpack.

"My aunt said I could invite you and your mom over to watch the fireworks. You like hot dogs?" he asked. "And s'mores?"

"I've never had one."

DJ threw his hand over his heart and fell to his knees on the ground. "You've never had a hot dog? That's insanity!"

I laughed. "No, a s'more."

DJ's shocked expression deepened. "Even weirder," he said. "So. Want to come?"

"I'll ask my mom," I said. "Sounds fun."

DJ scrambled back to his feet and handed me one of his rocks.

"I thought you might want to borrow it. For swim lessons tomorrow. For luck."

I rubbed the quartzite between my fingers. It was his good one, with the extra stripes and jagged edge. The one he'd found with his parents, and he was trusting it to me.

"Don't you need it?"

DJ's face flamed up. "It's okay. Just don't lose it."

"I won't," I said. "I promise."

DJ started to turn away, then paused. "I think she's good strange," he said. "Do you?"

"Charlotte? Yeah."

"I also think she thinks there's going to be an actual audience for her show. I mean, besides us. The way she made us rehearse so much? How bizarre is that? Who would she invite?"

Maddy Quinn. Kurt. Julie. I almost blurted it out and told him the truth. That there really was going to be an audience. But we'd worked so hard, and I was so close to completing my plan. I knew DJ wouldn't want to perform for Maddy. If I told him, then he might not show up. That would ruin the whole thing.

"She likes the extra drama?" I suggested.

"I don't care, it's fun," DJ said. "Anyway. Smell ya later!"

That night, I opened my notebook and took a close look at my Action Plan:

1. Meet Potentials
2. Narrow In
3. Develop Trust
4. Discover Her Secret Dream
5. Do What It Takes: Become the person who can make that dream come true!

I re-read the quote from the article Mom had given me. "You'll no longer have a client, you'll have a True Blue Friend for life—guaranteed!"

I unfolded Maddy's drawing of the poor fish getting eaten alive by a scary, scary mermaid. But that was only one scenario. On the other half of the page, the fish had a heart of gold and a best friend. It all depended on what happened next. The comic couldn't be clearer. Maddy

Quinn was trying to send me a message: I had Potential. She *wanted* to be my friend. She *would've* been my friend, but then I snooped in her closet and broke her trust. Of course she didn't know if I was True or False. Which was why I had to Do What It Takes to earn back her trust. I had to prove to her I was True.

I opened a new page in my notebook and wrote out an invitation:

COME SEE THE SPECTACULAR BOULAY MERMAID!
A MAGICAL EVENING YOU WON'T WANT TO MISS!!
JULY 4th—ONE NIGHT ONLY!!!!
Meet on the Showboat dock after the fireworks
100% SATISFACTION—GUARANTEED!!!!!!

I folded the note into a small square and tucked it in my backpack with DJ's quartzite and Josh's floaties. I climbed into bed and read a comic where Wolverine's past self travels into the future. The real-time Wolverine is old and losing his powers and he's not sure how to do the right thing, but he still ends up a hero because his younger self is willing to do anything—even manipulate the space-time continuum—to make sure he stays loyal to the bitter end.

30

SWIM LESSONS: TAKE THREE

I left my towel and backpack with Mom and marched down to the water, doing my best to pretend everyone wasn't staring at me. I started to visualize myself on a vast, empty beach with no spectators . . . then I stopped. Let them look. It was my last swim lesson, and I was going to make it count.

Before I put my feet in the water, I adjusted the SpongeBob SquarePants floaties on my arms. DJ's goggles made the whole world greenish blue. Thunder Lake was almost purple, like a washed-out photograph, and the kids running around in the weekly water fight looked sickly with their pale-blue skin.

It wasn't hard to spot DJ leaping around in the water with his arm stuck in the black garbage bag. He ran over, splashed water at my knees, and said, "You look like a bug-eyed mutant."

I splashed him back. "So? You look like a one-armed gorilla."

DJ raised his bagged cast in the air and yelled, "Tadpoles . . . charge!"

All at once, a gaggle of kindergartners came running at me, kicking and splashing. They chased me in thigh-high water while DJ jumped around like a zoo animal behind them.

"Attack the bug-eyed mutant!" he yelled. "Attack! Attack!"

The water was cold, but I didn't have time to care; I was too busy fending off the miniature army. I watched DJ and saw that he got a much bigger splash when he held his fingers close together and skimmed his hand across the water. I tried it and got Josh in the back of the head. He spun around, laughing, and smacked the surface of the lake with the palm of his hand. Water spattered around us.

"Watch this, Gills," DJ yelled.

He took a wide stance, held his good arm out, and made a wide sweep along the top of the lake. A wall of water seemed to fly through the air in slow motion before it hit me full in the face. I staggered, lost my footing, and fell backward. I felt my head go under before my butt hit the ground, and the floaties popped me back up to the surface. It all happened so fast. First I saw bubbles and then I was gasping for air and DJ was calling, "Time-out! Time-out!"

He reached his hand out for me while the blue-skinned Tadpoles gathered around. I took a breath. Surprisingly, I was okay. I hadn't swallowed any water. I wasn't down long enough to panic. But DJ looked terrified.

"I'm sorry," he said. "I didn't mean to . . . I wasn't thinking . . ."

I took his hand and let him help me up. Then I yelled, "Attack the one-armed gorilla!"

Josh chased after DJ, and the squealing army of kindergartners mobilized behind him. We ran, yelling and laughing, until Mrs. Nueske blew the whistle for lessons. As DJ unwrapped the plastic from his cast and headed to the beach, I saw Maddy Quinn watching me. She stood with the other Muskies, and her face was twisted into a strange greenish-blue expression. Even with the goggles on, I recognized it. Maddy Quinn thought I was a complete goon.

Shari handed out foam kickboards. "Anthoni, aren't you kind of big for floaties?"

"They help her feel safe," Josh said. "Right, Anthoni?"

I straightened up and turned away from Maddy's gaze. "That's right," I said, and smiled at him.

We practiced kicking, and then we practiced kicking

with our heads in the water. Shari said we were supposed to turn our heads to the side to breathe, but every time I tried it, I felt like I was going to drown, so I developed my own method. I'd lift my head straight up to the sky, gasp for air, and then duck my chin down, all the while kicking like my life depended on it. It wasn't Olympic style, but it worked. I was moving, and I was putting my head in the water.

I watched the bottom of the lake underneath me as I kicked, taking an inventory of everything I saw. Sand, weeds, minnows, Shari's hot-pink toenails. I sped past them all, gasping and ducking, gasping and ducking.

The Muskies had finished early and were already drying off on the beach when we came in from the lake. I grabbed my backpack and towel and joined the group.

"Nice floaties," Kurt said.

Josh shook his head like a dog and sprayed water all over him.

"You're doing pretty good for someone who never swam before," Julie said. Her poison ivy was hardly noticeable anymore. "You haven't drowned once. I bet those junior lifesavers are pretty glad, because they've never had to save anyone for real yet. I don't even know if they . . ."

She stopped talking the minute I handed the invitation over to Maddy.

"I can show you the mermaid," I said. "But I need to give her something in return."

A pang of guilt twitched through me as I said it. Technically, Charlotte wasn't a mermaid. But she was going to swim and breathe underwater, wasn't she? I was going to show Maddy what she wanted to see. That wasn't exactly lying.

"Give her what?" Maddy asked.

"The mermaid pin on your lamp."

Maddy's jaw tightened. I wasn't sure she'd forgiven me for snooping in her closet, and bringing it up was risky. But I'd promised Charlotte I'd get her the pin.

"You showed her our *pin*, too?" Julie turned to me. "Maddy and I found that together at the Wild Beach. We used to pretend it had magical powers that could help us find mermaids, but we never really found anything. Though once we did find some purple scales and my dad said they weren't from any fish *he* knows." She poked Maddy's arm. "Don't you remember that? Anyway. We'll have to give her something else. Maddy can't give that away."

"Please? I really need . . ." I started, and then I remembered the line from Action Step Three: *Don't bee needy; find a way to bee needed.* I tried to sound more confident. "I have to have the pin or I can't show you the mermaid."

"You can have it," Maddy said, avoiding Julie's eyes. "*After* we see the mermaid."

Julie looked hurt, but she tried to shake it off. She

put on a brave smile and tapped the invitation in Maddy's hand.

"It's good timing," she said. "We always watch the fireworks at Maddy's and walk Kurt home after. He lives next to DJ, who lives next to The Showboat, so we can see the mermaid and then go back to Maddy's for the sleepover. Don't forget to bring your pajamas. I got new ones with owls and polka dots. What are yours like?"

Sleepover? My heart did a skip.

Kurt shot Maddy a look of disbelief. "You invited Gills to your Fourth of July party?" he asked.

Maddy ignored him and smiled at me. "Your mom already said you can come," she said.

I sucked in my breath, and as if I were seven years old, I felt destiny closing in all around me. It was going to work. In my mind, my plan played out like a movie on the big screen. Fireworks, the Boulay Mermaid, then a sleepover. A sleepover. In Maddy's room with Storm and Emma Frost looking down on us. It was almost too perfect.

"So if this thing's real, you get some dumb pin," Kurt said. "What do *we* get? If you *can't* show us a mermaid?"

"Pride?" I offered lamely.

"Nah. How about you swim out to Maddy's raft?"

"With floaties?" Julie asked, but Maddy looked thoughtful. I could practically see her weighing the options: Is Gills True or False?

"I told you I don't like liars," she said. "If she's lying, no floaties. Sink or swim."

I didn't know what made me want to vomit more—the thought of swimming to Maddy's raft or the possibility of coming this close to a True Blue Friend only to end up in Maddy's False category. It was time to double down. Do What It Takes. I forced myself to remember the day in the boat, when the real Maddy—the nice Maddy—and I laughed until our sides hurt and she told me her secrets about Lexie. How happy I felt. How happy I was *going* to feel.

"Fine," I said.

"Swear it," Kurt said. "Out loud."

Maddy and I linked pinkies.

"I, Maddy Quinn, swear to give Anthoni my pin if she shows us a mermaid."

Maddy's pinkie grip was like a vise. I tried to ignore the fact that I was losing circulation in my fingertip. In my head, I chanted, *It Doesn't Matter If You Feel Brave; It Matters If You* Act *Brave*.

"I, Anthoni Gillis, swear to swim to the raft—without floaties—*if* Maddy does not see a mermaid. Which she will."

Maddy released my pinkie from her death-squeeze. Her eyes glinted with excitement.

"All right, see you on the Fourth," she said. "Be there

at four o'clock. My dad's barbecuing and we'll have sparklers."

They walked away and I bent down to zip up my backpack. When I stood up, DJ was in front of me.

"Hey!" I said, relieved to see him. "Want to go . . ."

But the color had drained out of his face, leaving his freckles no place to hide. I didn't know how much he'd heard, but clearly, he'd heard enough.

"I . . . it's not . . ."

"I told you not to tell Maddy about the mermaid," he said.

"I know, but . . ."

"You can't swim to the raft on your own," he said, anger forcing his face to flush again. "It's deep at Maddy's house. And it's far!"

"I won't have to," I said, though I wasn't as certain as I wanted to be. "It'll be fine."

"No. It won't!" DJ snapped. "In case you forgot, we don't *have* a mermaid. We have an old lady and some ancient breathing-tube system that probably doesn't even work."

I forced my voice to sound like Mom's Chief Pollinator voice—calm, cool, and collected. "People see what they want to believe," I said. "And Maddy Quinn wants to believe in mermaids."

DJ shook his head. "What are you doing? I thought

we were putting on the show for Charlotte, not to show off to a bunch of kids who don't even like us."

Lake water from my hair dripped down my back. I shivered. "They do too like us. Maddy's my friend. Well, she's going to be."

"Really? Are you sure about that?" DJ's anger dissipated and his shoulders sagged. "It doesn't matter. She's not a mermaid, Gills. She's just a lonely lady, and all they're going to do is make fun of her. You know that, don't you?"

"I . . ."

DJ waved his cast at me. "Whatever. Have fun watching the fireworks with your friends. I hope they have s'mores."

S'mores. I'd been so wrapped up in my plan that I'd forgotten about DJ's invitation to watch the fireworks and eat s'mores. My teeth chattered and I felt a headache coming on. I realized I was still wearing the blue goggles. I pulled them off, but after the blue tint, the whole world seemed blindingly yellow. The sun shot rays straight into my eyeballs. I rubbed them with my palms and blinked away the dark spots, glad for an excuse not to watch DJ turn around and walk away.

31
FIREWORKS

I gripped DJ's rock carefully between my fingers while Mom and I waited on the Quinns' magazine-perfect doorstep. Even though I wasn't sure the quartzite had any real luck in it, it had survived millions of years and been pressed to its limit, and after all that, it came out stronger on the other end. I felt better holding on to it. Like as long as I kept my head up, there was a sliver of hope that the plan could still work, and I could find a way to make everyone happy all at once, and DJ would forgive me for ditching him to go to a barbecue with a bunch of kids who didn't want him around.

It was worth a shot.

Mrs. Quinn held the door open wide.

"Anthoni! Carrie! We're glad you could come!" She

patted me on the head. "Get your suit on, hon. All the kids are down by the lake."

I changed into my suit in Maddy's room. I took a long look at Storm and Emma Frost before I tucked DJ's quartzite into the front pocket of my backpack, put on Josh's floaties, and propped DJ's goggles on top of my head. Then, even though I knew better, I peeked into Maddy's closet. The mermaid pin was still on the lamp, but all the stuffed animals had been cleared out. There wasn't a single dolphin in sight.

As I came down the stairs to the lake, Julie jumped up and down and waved at me.

Mr. Quinn chuckled. "Hey, Little Gills, we have life jackets, you know. You don't need those things."

"I like them," I said. "But I'll take a life jacket, too, please."

I sat in the boat and watched Maddy and Julie do a double trick-ski routine. Mr. Quinn set up two ropes, and they skied at the same time, doing 180s together like dancers or synchronized swimmers. Maddy didn't look bored like she did the last time I saw her ski. She and Julie grinned through the whole thing, slapping hands when they got a move just right and laughing when they turned at the wrong time. Once, they tried to link arms, and Julie's ski knocked into Maddy's, sending them flying into the water. When we turned around to pick them up, they were laughing so hard, they couldn't even hold the ropes Mr. Quinn tossed out to them.

It cheered me up to learn that Kurt was not a great skier. It took him four tries to get up, and when he did, he skied on two regular skis with a hunched back and wobbly knees. He fell twice, and the second time, instead of trying again, he climbed into the boat and we had to drive him back to the dock. I expected him to be embarrassed or upset, but he gave us all a double thumbs-up, and Mr. Quinn said, "Nice improvement, Kurt. We'll get all the way around the lake next time!"

When we pulled up to the dock, Mr. Quinn went into the boathouse and rolled out a flat disc of wood slightly bigger than a Hula-Hoop. "This is a treat for you, Little Gills," he said. "We'll get you behind the boat one way or another."

My heart stopped. I didn't *want* to get behind the boat. I thought of Mom, somersaulting through the air and plunging deep into Thunder Lake.

"Oooh, the saucer!" Julie squealed. "You'll love it, Anthoni."

Maddy smiled one of her sparkly, real-Maddy smiles, and Kurt said, "Anyone can do the saucer. Even you."

It was weird that everyone had been nice to me so far. It crossed my mind that they might be setting me up. The saucer could be a dangerous torture device—part of

233

a secret plan to dump me in the middle of the lake. On the other hand, I didn't believe Julie was capable of lying, and it seemed unlikely that Mr. Quinn would be in on it, too.

"How does it work?" I asked.

"Why don't we go together?" Mom appeared on the dock and did a cannonball into the water, spraying everyone in sight.

She steadied the saucer as I lay belly-down on top of it. I felt like the cheese on a giant, wooden pizza, only I kept slipping off. Mom put her weight next to me, throwing the disc off balance, and I shrieked. She laughed and threw her arm around me, steadying the saucer and holding me in place.

"We'll hold the rope together, and you yell 'Hit it!' when you feel ready to go."

I didn't think I'd ever feel ready to go. What if I couldn't keep hold of the rope? What if Mom couldn't keep us steady? I thought about DJ's quartzite in my backpack upstairs—stronger under pressure. I braced myself and yelled.

"Hit it!"

The boat accelerated, jerking my arms and lifting the front half of the saucer up above the water. My feet dragged behind, but my upper body was lifted by the pull of the rope. Julie cheered from the boat, and Mr. Quinn turned around and gave us a wave.

"Watch where you're going!" I shouted into the wind, but Mr. Quinn made a motion to show that he couldn't hear me, then faced forward and continued to drive.

The wind whipped into my face as I bounced and rocketed over the water. I was flying. I felt my lips spread into a smile.

Mom gave me a squeeze. "Feel good?" she shouted.

I nodded.

"Try this," she said. "I've got you."

She helped me scoot myself higher on the board and pull my legs up into a kneeling position. Mom got up on her knees behind me, her arms wrapped around mine, holding me safe and close. Sitting up like that, I had a better view of the houses and docks zooming past us. As we turned the corner near the bay, I watched The Showboat Resort drift past. The cabins, tucked into the trees, were barely visible at all. I squinted, hoping for a glimpse of Charlotte or DJ, but the dock was empty, and before I knew it, we were past the bay and back at Maddy's house.

After skiing, I stuffed myself with brats and potato salad and watermelon, and we made s'mores down by the lake—crisp graham crackers with gooey marshmallow-chocolate filling. It would have been the most delicious thing I'd ever tasted except that every time I took a bite, I thought about DJ eating s'mores alone with his aunt.

"Don't you like it?" Mom looked shocked as I handed her half a s'more.

"I'm full," I said.

And then the fireworks started up.

I'd seen plenty of fireworks before—bigger, flashier displays with more color and higher arcs—but Mom had been right. I hadn't seen anything like this.

It started at the public beach. A high-pitched squeal and then a crackling burst of blue light. As soon as the blue faded away, someone two docks down lit Roman candles. While they shot into the air, Mr. Quinn ran to the end of his dock and set off a tall fountain of white sparks. One by one, small fireworks began to launch from houses and cabins all around Thunder Lake. I hardly knew where to look. The sky sparkled from all sides, and as the sparks cascaded down toward the water, the surface of the lake glowed.

It lasted a few minutes, then the sky went black and a hush settled in across the lake. When it became clear that nothing else was coming, that the last firework had been lit, a cheer rose up in the darkness. All around the lake, people began to clap and whistle. Maddy and Julie screamed their heads off, and Mom and I stood up on our feet and shouted, "Wooooo!"

Even though I couldn't see any of the other cheerers, and even though I didn't know who most of them were,

I felt like an invisible string had been wound all around Thunder Lake, binding us together. Somewhere out there, Mrs. Nueske was clapping, and Shari, and all the Tadpoles, and the lady with the giant sunglasses. The sparkly-suit tanning girls were clapping, and DJ was clapping with his aunt. Maybe Charlotte Boulay was watching from the window of The Showboat, only maybe she wasn't clapping because she was thinking about other Fourth of Julys and the weight of the past and the mother she lost when she was twelve.

At the thought of Charlotte, the cozy, post-fireworks feeling disappeared. Was I really setting her up to be the butt of a mean joke?

Mom pushed a lock of hair behind my ear and whispered, "I'm glad we stayed for the fireworks. You were right."

"I might not want to stay overnight," I said.

"Okay," Mom said. "You can call me. But I bet you'll have more fun than you think." She glanced at Mrs. Quinn, who was picking up sticks and chocolate wrappers around the campfire. Mom leaned into me, tired. Or sad.

"You should take a vacation," I said. "Just for today. Have fun and don't worry about Beauty & the Bee."

Mom's mouth turned up a little. She patted my leg. "In that case, I think I'll go make another s'more."

As Mom walked over to Mrs. Quinn, Maddy came up behind me and grabbed my wrist. "Mom," she said loudly. "Kurt has to go now. Can we walk him home?"

"Don't stay too late," Mrs. Quinn said. "I don't know how 'walking Kurt home' always turns into a two-hour video-game spree. I want you home by nine."

"No video games. I promise," Maddy said, and squeezed my wrist again. "Everybody ready?"

"In a minute. I need something," I said.

I ran up to the house and grabbed my backpack. I put DJ's lucky rock in the pocket of my shorts and patted it, feeling a little stronger. As I closed the backpack, something caught on the zipper. It was the corner of the faded pink envelope DJ and I had found hidden in the back of the Boulay Mermaid photo. I knew I was dragging my feet, killing time, but I opened the flap and glanced through the collection of obituaries. Each one had a glamorous picture of smiling Selina Boulay. Selina in an evening dress, Selina in a fancy hat, Selina blowing kisses to the camera. The newspapers felt old and crumbly, and I wondered who had clipped and collected them all those years ago. Charlotte? Or was it Mr. Boulay?

As I placed the articles back into the envelope, I noticed one last clipping. It was a small square tucked into the corner. I unfolded it. This article was dated after Selina's death—August 19, 1942—and it showed a photo of Charlotte's dad standing outside The Showboat Resort.

COURT PULLS PLUG ON BOULAY MERMAID SHOW:
Ingenious Underwater Breathing Apparatus Deemed
Too Dangerous for Use

I read the article three times through, but my eyes skipped to the same lines. *Investigation launched . . . Selina Boulay strayed to an unrehearsed path . . . tangled rope and pulley system.*

I read the last line until it had been burned into my brain: *Due to the potential dangers involved, the Wisconsin State Court has ordered that the Boulay Mermaid act be shut down. Effective immediately.*

Potential dangers.

Too dangerous for use.

"Hey! Are you coming or what?"

I practically jumped out of my skin. Maddy Quinn stood in the bedroom door, waving me forward. I felt dizzy as I put the envelope away, but I shrugged my backpack onto my shoulders and followed Maddy out the door. I told myself Charlotte wouldn't agree to do the show if she thought it was dangerous. Of course she'd fixed the system—1942 was a long time ago. Breathing-tube technology had probably come a long way since then. I tried to focus on happy thoughts. *Fireworks. Charlotte Boulay dressed like a mermaid. Energy. Laughs. Applause. Maddy getting her socks knocked off. Charlotte on cloud nine. DJ smiling and turning red.*

But the happy thoughts kept disappearing underneath thoughts of Selina Boulay and Thunder Lake. All I could think of was how scary it would feel to be below that glassy surface, tied up in ropes, gasping for air, and no one on earth even knowing you were there.

32

OUT WITH A BANG

Maddy wore a headlamp and led us down a mosquito-infested path through the woods.

"You're sure this leads to The Showboat?" I asked.

"Of course, silly," Julie chirped. "We live here, don't we? This path is for snowmobiles in the winter, and it's a lot faster than driving because in a car you have to stick to the roads, but this is a straight shot. I've only used it to walk to Kurt's, not to The Showboat, because who would ever go to The Showboat? I mean, except you. Which is cool."

The woods were especially creepy at night—too quiet and dark to be safe—but no one else seemed to notice. I walked into something tickly that stuck to my arms and made my skin crawl. I danced around trying to shake it off, and Kurt shone the flashlight in my face.

"Relax, it's a spiderweb," he said. "Jeez. Freak out much?"

"I can't believe your parents let you do this," I said.

"Do what?" Julie asked. She hopped up onto a stump and hopped off.

"Walk in the woods at night."

"You're funny, Anthoni," Julie said. "What could happen?"

"*Everything!*" I said.

Maddy hooted like I'd said something hilarious. "*Nothing* happens in Eagle Waters."

"Shhh!" Julie leaned toward me. "We have to be quiet now because this is Kurt's house. His mom will freak if she finds out we're sneaking around, and then she'll call my mom, and my mom will call Maddy's mom . . ."

Kurt hit her in the arm. "Then shut up!"

The lights in the windows let out a reassuring glow, and I felt a little calmer. We weren't lost. We weren't completely disconnected from civilization. We passed a second house, and Julie whispered, "DJ and his aunt live there. But I bet you already know that."

I rubbed the quartzite in my pocket and tried to look in the windows, but the shades were drawn. I wondered if DJ was inside. Was he going to show up at the dock? I'd left him a note on The Black Bear after swimming lessons, and later, I found it crumpled on the ground. What if Charlotte didn't show either? She'd said she'd leave the lights on at The Black Bear and that would be the signal she was at her mark and ready to go. Part of me hoped she would change her mind and decide to scrap the whole thing. It would probably be for the best.

We followed a bend in the path, and finally I could see the windows of The Black Bear through the trees. They were filled with yellow light! From outside, the kitchen looked warm and cozy. I could see the butterfly sun catchers hanging above the sink and DJ's rocks spread out on the picnic table. The lights meant Charlotte was ready, and I was supposed to get into costume and give DJ the sign to turn on the spotlight.

Except DJ wasn't there.

I kept walking, but DJ wasn't by the spotlight either. I stood at the top of the stairs and peered down to the dock. The moon was behind a cloud, making the pine trees around the lake look thicker and darker than usual.

"Hello?" I called down the stairs. "We're not going to do it. DJ's not here."

Julie gasped. "What? We came all the way here. We have to do it!"

"Boo-hoo . . . DJ the Weird isn't here," Kurt said. "Why do we care about *that* mess?"

I almost shoved him. It was like a switch went off and all of the sudden, I'd had it with Kurt and his mean jokes. I wished I could morph into diamond form and knock him to the ground so hard the smirk would fall right off his face. Instead, I exploded.

"DJ's not a mess! He's the nicest person here, and if you weren't such a jerk, you might notice that he's also smart and funny, and I'd rather hang out with him than you *any* day of the week!"

I clenched my teeth. Julie sucked in her breath and Maddy gaped at me like I *had* knocked him out.

"I . . ." Kurt opened his mouth and closed it again. He looked weird. Embarrassed, or . . . sorry?

"Holy cow." Maddy whistled through her teeth. "She broke Kurt's snark machine!"

A voice hissed in the darkness. "Places!"

"What was that?" Maddy flashed her headlamp around the dock. A shadowy figure cloaked in black sat on the edge.

"Places!" the voice hissed again. It meant I was supposed to go to my mark and start the show.

"But I don't think we should . . ."

"Places! Spotlight! NOW!"

I didn't know what else to do. Charlotte was ready. Waiting for the finale she'd been preparing all week. I couldn't walk away and leave her sitting on the dock alone. Until I could think of something, forward seemed like the only direction to go.

Reluctantly, I unzipped my backpack and tied the cape around my neck. I set the top hat on my head.

"Julie," I said. "Want to run the spotlight?"

I showed her the numbers that marked the spotlight angles. "Whatever number she shouts out, move it to that spot."

"Who?" Julie whispered. "Who's shouting?"

"Char . . . the mermaid," I said. "Start it here." I turned on the light and tilted it toward the spot on the stairs where I was supposed to stand.

"This is so exciting!" she whispered.

I led Maddy and Kurt to the wooden bleachers. The dread I'd been pushing down was fogging up my brain. I felt like I was sleepwalking and my tongue weighed a thousand pounds. But I walked into the spotlight half-way down the stairs, and threw my arms wide like we'd rehearsed.

"Ladies and gentlemen," I said, taking a deep bow. "You are about to see something so specTACular, so aMAZing, that you won't believe your eyes."

I couldn't remember the next line. I froze. Maddy giggled, and as hard as I tried, I couldn't hold back the flood of Negative Thoughts. *DJ was right. This is a terrible idea. The plan is going to fail, they're going to make fun of Charlotte, and I am going to lose my last chance with Maddy Quinn.*

But my next thought hit me like a pile of bricks: *Who cares?*

I stuck my hand in my pocket, touched DJ's quartzite, and thought it again: *WHO CARES?* So what if Maddy liked comics and had a smile that made you feel all tingly? A True Blue Friend wouldn't make fun of you in front of her friends. She wouldn't dare you to swim to a raft when she knew you couldn't do it. If she really liked you, she wouldn't ask you to do something dangerous. Unless it was important. Like saving the planet from a meteor attack. Or helping a friend escape from Mr. Sinister's lair. A True Blue Friend had your back. Always.

It was that simple. Charlotte was my friend and I was asking her to do something dangerous. I remembered Mom's words during our fight: *Sometimes you have to know when to give up on a plan.*

I unzipped my backpack and took out Josh's floaties.

"I'll swim to the raft," I said, snugging the floaties up onto my arms. "I made it all up. There's no mermaid. We'll go back right now, and I'll swim to the raft."

Kurt groaned, but Maddy looked lost. Sad, even. Then she pulled herself together. "I knew you were lying!" she said in her snarkiest evil-Maddy voice. "Let's go. And I said no floaties. You swore it."

"Fine," I said, but I couldn't bring myself to take them off.

Charlotte's voice bellowed into the darkness. "ZIP IT!" she boomed. "What a bunch of ninnies. You are *ruining* the effect!"

"Who *is* that?" Maddy asked, pointing her headlamp toward the cloaked figure again.

"What do you think introductory remarks are for?" Charlotte asked, exasperated. "*Introductions!* Now sit down and shut up! Spotlight two!"

We stood in silence, and she yelled it again. "I said, *spotlight two!*"

"Oh! Me!" Julie squeaked.

The spotlight moved shakily to the dock, and the shadowy figure dropped her cloak, revealing the Boulay Mermaid. She sat on the edge, smiling and waving at her audience like nothing at all unusual had happened. Her orange hair was held back by a butterfly headband, and her face was painted with thick makeup—gaudy red lipstick that matched the round circles of rouge on her cheeks. She wore a bikini top that made the skin under her arm look especially flabby—it waggled as she waved. Her body seemed impossibly white and wrinkled in the light. But I couldn't take my eyes off the tail. Huge and green, it hung over the dock into the water, shimmering in the spotlight. The Boulay Mermaid looked spectacular.

Maddy sucked in her breath and sat down.

Charlotte lifted her tail and flopped it back into the water. She smiled at her audience and waved her hands in some sort of seated mermaid dance. Then, without warning, she dove.

Nobody moved a muscle.

We heard a splash of water before we heard her call out, "Spotlight three!"

Julie shone the light on a spot farther out in the lake. The Boulay Mermaid did some more arm dancing. Then, she jumped like a dolphin into the air, flashed her tail, and dove back down. Maddy gasped, and I sat down on the stairs, mouth open. How did she *do* that?

At spot four, the Boulay Mermaid did two dolphin dives and another twirly arm dance.

At spot five, she was out too far for us to see much, but we heard some splashing until she dove down again, and it was quiet. The moon came out from behind the clouds and the white light twinkled on the water. My body felt like it was standing on another planet. Like I'd been transported into a completely new world where anything was possible. Including magic. Including mermaids.

Kurt spoke first. "Where did she go?"

I stared out at the water and the feeling of wonder evaporated. She'd been down a lot longer than she had been between spots two and three, but from the window seat of The Blue Heron, I'd seen her stay down impossibly long. She was probably trying to play up the suspense.

"Do you think she's all right?" Julie asked loudly.

"Of course," I said. But my voice wavered. "Try scanning the spotlight. Are you on the right number?"

Julie moved the spotlight along the water, then abruptly stopped.

"Anthoni! There's a rope moving at my feet! And I'm not even touching it."

The emergency line.

I felt sick. Charlotte said it was just a safety precaution—we'd never have to use it, but we had to know how it worked. If she got in trouble (which she wouldn't), she'd pull it and we could send for help.

Everything seemed wrong and out of focus. My heart beat like it wanted to escape from my chest. I felt Maddy's fingers on my arm as I untied the cape from my neck. Her eyes were shining.

"I can't believe it," she whispered. "She's actually . . . swimming down there."

I brushed her hand away. The emergency line had been pulled. Whatever Charlotte was doing, it wasn't swimming.

As Julie scanned the lake with the light, my eye caught something not far from the dock. A bubble? A flash of hair?

"There!" I shouted. "Julie! Stop there! Somebody go get my mom."

As I ran down the stairs, I heard footsteps behind me. I could have sworn I saw DJ as I threw the top hat onto the dock and jumped into Thunder Lake.

33

SPLASH! TAKE THREE

G ills!"
    I heard DJ shout, but it was too late. I was in
the water, kicking like crazy toward the spotlight. I
guess when I jumped, I expected to feel like Storm, taming the waters in an act of daring heroism. But as I kicked,
panic settled in. The water was pitch-black, and the spotlight lit the surface with an eerie white glow. I couldn't
see Charlotte. I couldn't see anything. The floaties helped
me stay above water, but my shorts and T-shirt felt like
deadweights pulling me down.

Even if I found her, what was I planning to do?

I heard a splash, and the next thing I knew, DJ was
treading water beside me.

"Your cast! You'll ruin it."

DJ shook the water out of his eyes. "Better than watching you drown." He moved closer so I could put my hand on his shoulder for stability. I immediately felt lighter.

"Any sign of her?"

I shook my head. The panic was threatening to suffocate me.

"Come on, Gills," DJ said. "Come back to the dock. Kurt went to get help."

"I can't. It's my fault. I can't leave her here."

A lump swelled in my throat, and I swallowed it down. DJ tried to pull me back toward shore, but I kicked against him and we both started to sink.

"Maddy," DJ's voice sounded strained, almost like a growl. "Help me help Gills."

I looked back at the dock where Maddy stood, and I was surprised to see that I'd only gone about five feet. So much for power swimming.

Maddy hesitated.

"Now!" DJ yelled, and she jumped in the water with a splash. Off in the distance, a second splash echoed in the night air.

"I see her!" Julie yelled, and moved the spotlight several yards away from us. Charlotte's head bobbed in the white light, and she sputtered, looking disoriented and scared.

"We're coming!" I shouted.

I kicked furiously, ignoring my fear and trying to focus on one thing at a time. Swim to the spotlight. Help Charlotte. Swim back. The water was inky black, and I forced myself to remember that the only things below my feet were rocks and sand and minnows. Not water snakes. Not evil night serpents with teeth.

"Just reach out," DJ whispered at my side. "If you need help. We're here."

We swam closer and closer to the light and when it flooded around us, I could see Charlotte was treading water with one hand. Her thin hair was plastered to her head in wet clumps. The butterfly headband was gone, but her bright makeup was still perfectly intact. Her painted red cheeks glistened in the spotlight.

"I'm tangled," she said. "I got as close to shore as I could, but I can't move any farther."

Her left arm was pinned back by a thin rope that had wrapped itself tightly around her tail. She locked her eyes on mine.

"Well, what's the plan, Stan?" She asked it in a low, mobster voice, but her smile was pinched. Charlotte Boulay looked scared.

I tugged on the rope.

"It's really stuck," I said.

DJ and Maddy took turns pulling as we tried to untangle Charlotte's arm. It was no use.

"Julie!" Maddy yelled. "We need scissors! Or a knife!"

The spotlight wobbled as Julie let it go. What if it took too long? My legs were getting tired of kicking, and I'd already swallowed two mouthfuls of dark, fishy lake water. Even with the floaties, I didn't know how long I could keep it up. Charlotte seemed to be sinking lower and lower every minute. DJ pulled her free arm over his shoulder and the pinched look on her face relaxed.

"Hold on to me like that," I said to Maddy.

I draped one arm over her shoulder and struggled to get my other hand into my wet shorts. DJ's Baraboo Quartzite was still there. Stone Age humans used it as a tool—but was it sharp enough to cut rope?

I gripped the quartzite and sawed as hard as I could. Nothing happened.

I sawed harder. It *had* to work. I imagined the iron particles fused in the rock, like the adamantium fused to Wolverine's bones. He didn't let the scientists use him as a weapon. He turned himself into a hero instead.

One thread snapped, then another. I handed the stone to Maddy. She took a turn, then DJ. It seemed like we sawed at it for hours, the four of us treading water, holding on to one another for support, but in reality, it could only have taken a minute. The quartzite was sharp and each time a strand of rope broke, our hope grew and we sawed harder.

I was holding the rock when the last thread snapped. The shock of it made the stone slip from my hand. DJ's quartzite!

I let go of Maddy's shoulder and lunged for it. I felt the cold stone cut into my palm as I grabbed it, but I held on. I'd already made a disaster out of things. I couldn't bear to let DJ down one more time.

Charlotte wriggled herself free, stretched out her left arm, and let go of DJ, treading water with both arms now. She smiled weakly.

"That's the breaks, kids," she said. "Some days you eat the bear, some days the bear eats you."

She leaned her head to the side and started singing in a low, wobbly voice: "We'll meet again, don't know where, don't know when . . ."

It was the song that was supposed to be her finale number. The one she would sing right before one final, spectacular dive. Then the spotlight would flip off and the audience would go wild with applause, hooting and hollering, shouting for an encore. "Always be prepared for an encore," she'd said.

But now, her voice cracked, and she simply paused mid-song and side-stroked away from us. After a few strokes, she gave a tired jazz-hands wave, and dove. The tip of her tail flicked briefly to the surface. And then she was gone.

With Charlotte untangled, I was suddenly too tired to tread water anymore. Josh's floaties were still keeping my arms up, but my clothes dragged me lower, and another mouthful of water went down my throat. I tried to spit it out, but I only sucked in more. I started to sputter as reality sank in. What had I been thinking? I couldn't swim. We'd saved Charlotte, but now what? The murky water felt like it was closing in. It was freezing. How had I not noticed how cold I was?

DJ placed his shoulder behind my neck.

"You can do it," Maddy said. "Tip your head back. Relax. Just float and we'll help you to the dock. We're not far."

I leaned back and water rushed in my ears with a live, pulsing sound. I felt Josh's floaties and DJ's shoulder hold me up. Maddy put her hand under my back and they towed me to shore. When we got close enough, Maddy squeezed my arm.

"You can touch here," she said.

I let my feet sink to the bottom of the lake and stood. My legs felt like rubber and my entire body was covered in goose bumps. For a second, the world stood quiet and still, and then with a lurch, everything kicked into high speed. Julie ran down the stairs waving the pair of scissors we didn't need anymore. Seconds behind her, Mom and the Quinns showed up with Kurt, his mom, and DJ's aunt. We weren't even out of the water before the adults started talking a mile a minute. They didn't let us get a word in edgewise.

"What in the world, Anthoni? Kurt said you jumped in after a *mermaid?*"

"Who started this nonsense?"

"Julie, make-believe is fun, but swimming at night is dangerous."

"I don't care what you *thought* you saw. You are getting in the car and coming home."

I felt like everything was happening and not happening all around me. Like it was a dream or a play I was watching from a hundred miles away. DJ's aunt practically fainted when she saw his waterlogged cast. She dragged him up the stairs and down the path, and I couldn't make my mouth say anything. Thank you. Or goodbye. Julie went home with Kurt and his mom. I hardly noticed that someone took off my floaties and wrapped me up in a towel. I was so tired. I deserved to be tired. It was my fault. All my fault. Charlotte could have died because of me and my stupid plan.

Charlotte. With a burst of energy, I spun around.

"Where is she? Where's Charlotte?"

Mr. and Mrs. Quinn were the only ones left on the dock still talking with Maddy and Mom. All four of them seemed confused.

"Boulay? Probably in bed," Mr. Quinn said. "Like *we* should be."

I scanned the water and the shore. I'd thought she was swimming back. She was ahead of us. She should be here already. But she wasn't.

"Mom!" I cried. "Call an ambulance! Call somebody! We have to help her. What if she got tangled again? What if she's hurt?"

"Oh, sweetie." Mom made me sit down on the dock. She put her hand on my forehead. "I think you have a fever," she said. "And what happened to your hand?" She took the quartzite out of my palm and set it on the dock. The cut wasn't deep, but there was blood on my towel. "Come on, now, let's go home."

I looked out over the lake. The surface was smooth, reflecting the moon and stars like the whole night had been serene and calm. Like nothing bad had ever happened below the surface of Thunder Lake.

I pushed Mom's arms away and lay down, resting my head on the dock next to DJ's purple quartzite. The air in my lungs felt heavy. I didn't want to go back to the cabin. I didn't want to go anywhere. As I lay there, staring out at Thunder Lake, Charlotte's song echoed on repeat in my head. *We'll meet again, don't know where, don't know when* . . .

The tears rose fast and strong. The Boulay Mermaid was gone.

34

THE SHOW MUST GO ON

H ere."

I'd only been laying there a few seconds before I felt something metal being pressed into my good hand. It was a hairpin in the shape of a star, with a mermaid inside. I closed my fist around it.

"I'm sorry I called you a liar," Maddy said. Then she smiled. "Don't worry. She's untangled. She probably swam back to her home."

She didn't get it. Maddy Quinn was oblivious.

I sat up and stared at her. She had her nice-Maddy smile on. Her let's-be-friends smile. The kind of smile I would have done backflips for a few days ago. But now, it didn't look that different from any other smile. Nothing magical or Meant to Be. Just lips turned up into a grin. Charlotte had been right. People see what they want to believe. Including me.

"Good night, Maddy," Mom said, giving her a stern, you're-not-helping look. "Your mom's waiting."

Maddy turned to join her parents, and I heard her footsteps fade away on the stairs.

"You, too," Mom said. "Time to go."

I shook my head. "But Char—"

"Honey, I've never seen you like this. We need to get you to bed."

"Can I have two minutes? By myself."

I needed space to think, but Mom didn't move.

"Please?" I looked up at her and begged with my eyes. "I won't move from this spot, but I need to stay here. I can't go in right now."

She looked concerned, but her eyes softened. "Two minutes," she said. "I'll sit on the stairs and give you space for two minutes, but then we're going home, even if I have to carry you."

"Thanks," I said, staring at the hairpin in my hand.

The pin looked too delicate to survive underwater all those years. I unlatched it and clipped it onto my hair. The sobs started up again. I pictured Charlotte Boulay with her crooked tooth, dancing and singing in front of the Showboat hotel. *Out with a bang*, she'd said. *Our big finale.* The dock and the lake blurred behind my tears.

All Charlotte wanted was for someone to notice her. To look beneath the surface and really *see* her.

I had. DJ had. What we saw was that she wasn't just a kooky old lady. She was funny. And generous. Loyal. To the bitter end.

A cold hand rested on my shoulder.

"Don't cry, kid. We killed 'em tonight."

I looked up. Charlotte Boulay stood over me in a pink, shimmery sundress with elbow-length gloves and a feathery hat. There wasn't a trace of her gaudy makeup.

"Where were you?" I tried to shout, but my voice came out scratchy and raw. "I thought you drowned!"

Saying the words out loud unlocked a new floodgate of tears. Charlotte sat down cross-legged on the dock next to me, shimmery dress and all.

She winked at me. "Came up the side way. Didn't want to ruin the effect. The show must go on, and all that jazz."

She was chipper and energetic, like nothing had happened. If it wasn't for the red rope burn peeking out of the glove on her left arm, I would have thought I imagined the whole thing.

"Shhh, now. You shouldn't sob like that," she said. "It's bad for your voice. A performer with your talent needs a healthy set of cords."

I crinkled my forehead. I didn't know whether to

laugh or keep crying or yell at her. Charlotte Boulay was the most unpredictable human being I'd ever met in my whole life.

She laid her hand on my back, rubbing soothing circles and repeating "shhh now, shhh," until my breathing slowed and the tears dried up. A breeze blew across Thunder Lake, chopping up the surface and scattering the reflection of the moon. The light glittered on the water like thousands of tiny diamonds.

When I'd pulled myself together, I unclipped the hairpin and handed it to her.

"We got it back," I said.

Charlotte took the pin and gently turned it over, examining it like it was a rare jewel. Slowly, she brought it to her lips, kissed it, and with trembling hands, lifted it to her head.

"I can do it." I reached over and pinned the mermaid to her damp, fiery hair. The star glinted in the moonlight.

Charlotte raised her hands to the night sky. "We had a heck of a finale," she said. "No one's going to forget a couple of kooks like us." She made her hand into a fist, chucked me gently on the chin, then threw her head back and howled, "Yowzah, yowzah, yowzah!"

I couldn't help myself. I laughed.

"Hey, kid," Charlotte said.

"Yeah?"

"I was wrong. Some friends are true. They're just not always the ones you'd expect. Thanks for helping me."

I nodded and thought of DJ showing up in the nick of time when I needed him, brave as Storm or Wolverine, and Charlotte risking her life to help me with my plan to win a friend. The truth was, I'd had True Blue Friends staring me in the face all along. Not that it mattered anymore. Tomorrow I'd be in Chicago, starting from scratch with a new life.

"Hey, kid," Charlotte said again.

"Yeah?"

"You ever had a pen pal?"

"No."

"Did you ever *wish* you had one?"

"Always."

We sat in silence, and somewhere on the other side of the lake, one last firework went off. The sparks sputtered in the air before plummeting into the water, fizzing out into darkness.

35

TRUE BLUE

Mom and I finished packing the Beemobile in silence. Mom was depressed because she'd gone almost four weeks without checking off a single goal on her whiteboard. I was depressed because even though we'd stayed a few days past July Fourth, Mom made me spend those days in bed. I didn't have a fever, but she was convinced the whole mermaid incident meant I was having some kind of breakdown.

As far as I knew, she could be right. I'd let everybody down. Because of me, DJ had to get a new cast; Maddy, Julie, and Kurt all got grounded for sneaking out to The Showboat; and there were rumors that Charlotte Boulay was moving to a nursing home like Gramps. I had to learn all that news from Mom because I hadn't seen any of them since the Fourth. It was almost a relief that we were leaving. As usual, nobody was going to be sorry to see me go.

I went back into the cabin and put a few last things in my backpack: Josh's floaties, a perfect pinecone, and my Lady Alice and Boulay Mermaid photos. Then I flopped into a hanging chair for one last swivel. Mom set down a box and joined me.

"So . . ." She fiddled with the keys in her hand. "I had a conversation with your grandpa."

"Really?"

"I told him we'd stop and see him this weekend after we get settled in at Kimmy's. Shady Rest isn't too far from her neighborhood."

"Thanks, Mom," I said. "I've really missed him."

"I know. Me, too."

Something scratched at the screen door, but when I got up to look out, there was nothing on the porch except a pinecone. Then I heard a rustle of leaves and a soft "Meow."

I grabbed my backpack. "Hey, Mom . . . can I go out for a few minutes?"

She looked at the clock, recalculating.

"I know it'll put us behind schedule," I said. "If we plan to get to Chicago by . . ."

"The plan hasn't been helping us much, lately, has it?" Mom said. "Might as well do what we want. Take your time."

I found DJ on the stairs to the dock, looking out over Thunder Lake. His new cast was neon purple, and he held it above his forehead, shading his eyes from the sun. I braced myself in case he was mad and getting ready to yell.

"Hey," I said. "Can I sit here?"

He nodded. He didn't seem mad. Disappointed would be worse.

"Nice cast."

DJ held it up to his nose. "Smells fresh," he said. "Want a whiff?"

"That's disgusting."

DJ gave a half smile.

"I saw you guys packing the car."

"Yeah."

I opened my backpack and rummaged around until I found his jagged piece of quartzite. When I handed it to him, I was surprised to find my face burning as red as his.

DJ took the rock and put it in his pocket.

"You were right, DJ," I said. "About everything.

I should have listened. And . . ." My face burned even hotter, but I choked out the words anyway. "You're the truest friend here, and I ditched you. I don't blame you if you hate me, but . . ."

"I heard what you said to Kurt," DJ interrupted. "When he called me a mess."

"You did?"

"Yeah." DJ shot me a giant, triumphant grin. "You think I'm great!"

My cheeks felt like they were on fire. "How? You weren't even there."

"Sure I was. In the woods. Turns out camouflage works best at night."

He pumped his fist in the air, and I put my face in my hands, feeling happy and embarrassed and relieved all at the same time.

"Well, it's true," I said. "If I had a superpower, I'd use it to rewind the whole summer and start again. I'd even clean up your puke this time."

DJ fumbled in his pocket and pulled out a Ziploc bag. "Speaking of superpowers, I made you this."

Inside the bag was a necklace made of wire and a small, pale-pink piece of quartzite with a single purple band. There was writing on one side of the rock. In black Sharpie letters it said: *SNIKT!*

"*SNIKT?* Like Wolverine?"

DJ shrugged. "You said quartzite reminded you of him, so I looked him up. It's like his catchphrase or something?"

It wasn't a catchphrase. It was the sound Wolverine's claws made when they extended. Still, close enough. I was impressed.

"It's kind of ugly," DJ said. He was right. The wire was thick and misshapen, and there were fat globs of glue that had dried all over the rock.

I put the necklace on.

"It's perfect," I said.

I was about to tell him I didn't have anything for him, but then a brainwave hit me. I pulled my notebook out of my backpack and ripped out a list I'd been working on while I was stuck in bed.

"Here," I said. "You might as well have this."

TRUE BLUE FRIEND CRITERIA (revised)

1. Takes you seriously
2. Tells you when you're wrong
3. Doesn't judge people because they're strange
4. Is a little strange (in the best way)
5. Teaches you about new things (like geology & drown-proof research)
6. Knows ghost karate
7. Sticks by you when you're scared
8. Shows. Up. When. Needed.

It was DJ's turn to look embarrassed. As he read through the list, his face flamed up. At this rate, we were going to set off a fire alarm.

"Thanks, Gills."

We sat there, staring at the lake, while DJ folded the paper into smaller and smaller squares. When he couldn't fold it any more, he stood up and tucked it in his pocket with the quartzite.

"Well, it's been weird to know ya," I said.

"Are you coming back next summer?" DJ asked. "You should. We could get Charlotte to teach us her dance moves."

I knew he was joking about the dancing, but it actually sounded fun.

"I hope so," I said. "I'll try."

"Okay. See you next year, maybe."

"Maybe," I said. The word felt filled with Potential.

36

NEXT HIVE DESTINATION: CHICAGO, IL

Mom waited in the car while I ran inside the Showboat hotel. Charlotte was in the front office, hanging a new photo in the place where Lady Alice and her Dirty Rats had been. She wore a pair of overalls and a floppy straw hat. Behind her, an ancient poster I hadn't seen before hung above the desk.

THE SHOWBOAT RESORT
HOME OF THE SPECTACULAR
BOULAY MERMAID!

"Kid," she said, "you're just in time. Want to give it the old John Hancock?"

"The what?"

"Autograph. Yours."

She took down the photo she was hanging and removed it from the frame. It was a black-and-white picture of me and DJ standing at the spotlight, rehearsing for the Boulay Mermaid show. DJ was grinning, and even in black and white, I could tell his face was red. I was delivering my lines, arms outstretched, looking like a goon.

"When did you take this? I didn't see you do it."

Charlotte waggled her eyebrows at me. "The depths of my mysterious ways have yet to be plumbed," she said. "Mostly because plumbers are so expensive these days. Ba-dum-bum!"

She winked at me, and I took the pen from her hand and wrote, "To Charlotte Boulay. From your friend, Gills."

I handed it back to her. "I couldn't think of anything clever."

"'Friend' is good," Charlotte said. "I'll take it."

"Are you really moving to a nursing home?"

Charlotte tipped back her head and barked out a laugh. "Don't believe all the fish tales you hear, kid."

"Good," I said, and handed her a faded pink envelope. "I thought you might want this."

Charlotte pulled out the articles and spread them on the front desk. When she finally spoke, her voice was hushed. "Where did you find these?"

I waggled mysterious eyebrows right back at her. "You're right," I said. "She should have been in the movies."

Charlotte looked at the photos of her mom and smiled. It wasn't a pinched, sad, weight-of-the-past kind of smile. It was a full-on, right-now, glad-for-happy-memories grin.

"I've got something, too." Charlotte Boulay reached behind the desk and pulled out a wrapped box. "For you. Open it on the ride down to Chicago."

"Thanks." I waved to the mermaid lamp and opened the door.

"Hey, kid."

I turned. Charlotte looked small and frail behind the traveling trunks. The sunlight from the open door threw a soft glow around her hair, making it look less orange, making her look like a normal old woman, somebody's grandmother, about to be left all alone. Then she put a hand on the front desk for support, stepped up on her stool, and threw her arms wide.

"Anthoni Gillis!" she yelled at the top of her lungs. "Knock 'em dead out there!"

EPILOGUE

Dear Kid,

Enclosed, please find one box of Genuine, Grade-A, Pen-Pal-Letter-Writing Paper. This spectacular, one-of-a-kind stationery is Pure Genius. If you use it, you will write the most Fascinating, Jaw-Dropping, Tear-Jerking letters of All Time.

I look forward to receiving them.

Yours truly,
Charlotte Boulay

p.s. Enclosed, please also find an order for three cases of your mother's wondrous wrinkle-free elixir. Who knows? The stuff might work.

HOW TO PUBLISH A NOVEL IN FOUR EASY STEPS

All you need is the herculean support
of impossibly SPECTACULAR friends!

ACTION STEP 1: GATHER MATERIAL

I could not have written this book without: growing up
on a lake, hating swimming lessons, or tagging along
to Tupperware, Avon, Longaberger basket, Color Me
Beautiful, and other home parties of the 1980s. Or without
April, Amy, Katie, Matt, Andy, and Danyon Jay—True
Blue Friends when I needed them most. Living near a
once-famous resort with a boat-shaped lounge and having a family with generations of competition-level water-
skiers also helped.

ACTION STEP 2:
RESEARCH

I am indebted to *No Applause—Just Throw Money* by Trav S.D. and to PinkTruth.com. To the Three Lakes Historical Society & Museum, Carl Marty, and his Showboat Lounge. To the University of Wisconsin–Extension and Alan Vodicka for geology advice. To Carol Martin for rock knowledge (but really for saving my academic career). To Prof. Walton for everything from Marilynne Robinson to *The Clean Team*. All the childhood hours spent watching movies like *Ziegfeld Girl* (1941), *The Seven Little Foys* (1955), and *Singin' in the Rain* (1952), and especially the day I skipped school to watch the TCM Esther Williams marathon: totally worth it.

ACTION STEP 3:
CHOP WOOD (GIT 'ER DONE!)

Thank you to Kevin Johnson and Anna Vodicka for never letting me off easy. To generous readers and writers: Anthony Walton, Deborah Murphy, Ann Braden, Scott Johnson, Susan Olcott, the Richardson-Plueckers, the Chiappinellis, Kyle Beeton, Brian and Katie Quirk, Michele LaForge, Jim Adolf, Cynthia Lord, and Kate

Egan. To Chris Richman for seeing the Potential. To my editor, Grace Kendall, who truly is Queen Bee. To my agent, John Cusick—ventriloquist, medicine man, and trick bicyclist. And to the hardworking teams at FSG and Folio, Jr., who have put their time and talents into making this a real book, including but not limited to Elizabeth H. Clark, Jennifer Sale, Nicholas Henderson, Lauren Festa, Kylie Byrd, Jeff Freiert, Christina Dacanay, Lucy Del Priore, Brittany Pearlman, Melissa Zar, and Shivani Annirood. A standing ovation to artist Maike Plenzke for bringing Thunder Lake to vibrant Technicolor life.

ACTION STEP 4: CELEBRATE!

As a little kid, I claimed I was an author. My off-the-wall, gigantic family believed me. My whole life, they've been my cheerleaders, doing veritable backflips and water-ski pyramids for every slow-but-steady win (we always *did* think my Lead Shoe Award in track was symbolic). You guys are the BEST! Think we can finally use the catchphrase? Snailed It!